Ragna the Dragon Rider
A Time of Dragons III

by
Cynthia Vespia

RAYNA THE DRAGON RIDER

A Time of Dragons Volume III

Copyright © 2024 Cynthia Vespia

All rights reserved.

ISBN: 978-1-7376927-5-1

Cover Image: ID 152302724 ©Refluo | Dreamstime.com
Back Cover Image: ElixorDesigns on Etsy
Map Design by: AEKCreates on Etsy
Additional Cover Edits: Original Cyn Content

***The fierce dragon warrior faces her greatest foes
in a dance with source magic.***

She conquered kings, magical beasts, and witches of chaos. But Rayna's journey is not yet complete. Far from her home and wounded, Rayna learns a great threat has risen.

After a thousand years of slumber, The Source Gods have returned to the world they created to reclaim it. The very existence of humanity is at stake and only Rayna wields a power strong enough to save it.

But is having a dragon enough to stop the threat, or will facing off against the gods be Rayna's last stand?

A story of heroes, gods, and unyielding courage.

Rayna the Dragon Rider is the third book in an exciting dragon fantasy adventure series A Time of Dragons. A tale of betrayal, war, and survival that blends old characters and new in a richly imagined world.

CHAPTERS

A Time of Dragons Series

Rise of the Dragonslayer (*prequel*)
Rayna the Dragonslayer - book 1
Rayna the Dragon Warrior - book 2
Rayna the Dragon Rider - book 3

For the People of Maui

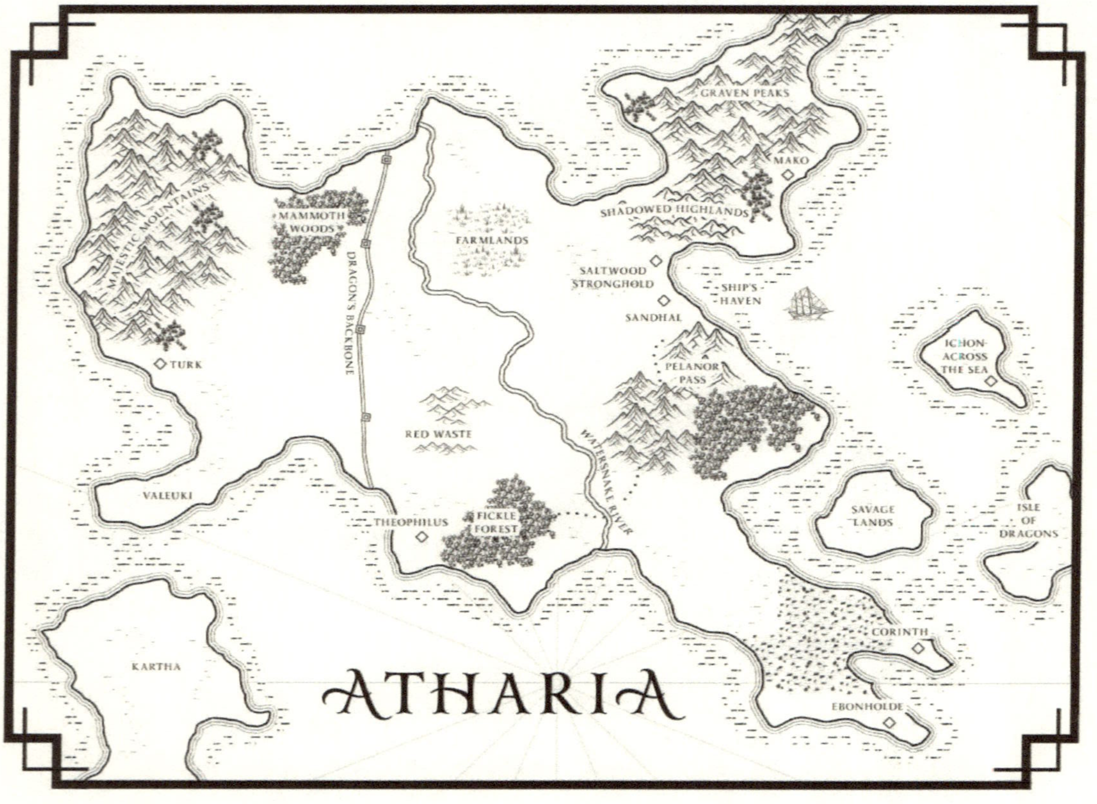
ATHARIA
MAJESTIC MOUNTAINS
MAMMOTH WOODS
DRAGON'S BACKBONE
FARMLANDS
GRAVEN PEAKS
MAKO
SHADOWED HIGHLANDS
SALTWOOD STRONGHOLD
SHIP'S HAVEN
SANDHAL
TURK
PELANOR PASS
ICHON-ACROSS THE SEA
RED WASTE
VALEUKI
WATERSNAKE RIVER
THEOPHILUS
FICKLE FOREST
SAVAGE LANDS
ISLE OF DRAGONS
KARTHA
CORINTH
EBONHOLDE

I
Flight of the Dragon

Ryu carried Rayna on his back for miles before his energy gave out. He started a downward spiral somewhere over the ocean. In Rayna's weakened condition all she could do was cling to the dragon's neck as they spun out.

Wind ripped through her hair and lashed across her wounds. She gritted her teeth and shut her eyes tight, overwhelmed with a sense of fear. Rayna never did like heights and plummeting towards the ocean out of control is exactly why.

Fortunately, Ryu managed one last push to keep them in the air. They came close enough to the water that his tail skidded across it. The cool splash over her skin roused Rayna enough so she could help steer Ryu towards land.

He jutted up across an expanse of desert that made

Rayna believe they were back at the Red Waste. But as he flew deeper into the island, she realized he'd brought them all the way down to Kartha.

Memories of her time there came back in a flash. Some good; mostly bad. Rayna tried to get Ryu to turn around and take them back to Atharia. She needed to find Jagger and K'lani. Promises were made to reunite at Theopilous after the war with the dragon queen ended. Rayna intended on keeping that promise to her husband.

Ryu would have none of it. He was weary from flying and the long time spent in captivity. Once they found themselves over land he didn't hesitate to touch down. Flying on the back of a dragon with a fear of heights is not something Rayna would ever get used to. When he finally landed, she rolled off his back and retched on the ground.

She took a moment to compose herself then searched the area. Ryu set them down in an obscure spot of the island near the beach. In the very least he'd set them down far enough away from the towns that they weren't immediately discovered. That wouldn't last long.

If anyone spotted the dragon in the sky, there would be an army headed for them in moments. Rayna tried to rally Ryu back into flight. He chuffed at her and turned his head.

"Come this is no time to be stubborn," she told him, almost pleading.

Ryu curled up beneath his wings intent on resting. Nothing Rayna did would rouse him. If anything, her constant commands only proved to irritate the dragon and he shouted in such a way it forced her to back off.

Rayna felt her own wounds starting to catch up with her as well. Battling a magical witch-turned-dragon left neither of them unscathed. She had an open gash upon her side where the dark dragon's tooth almost impaled her. It needed to get stitched up before she lost too much blood.

The barren surroundings didn't show anything useful to aide her. Instead, she would have to make a poultice to staunch the blood. That meant venturing further out. She hesitated before going; troubled by the thought of leaving Ryu by himself.

They'd been through a lot together. He'd become her best companion. A strange pairing of a once mighty dragon slayer and the last known child of dragon lineage. In a way, Ryu had become like her child now.

Rayna stroked his snout and tried to reassure him she wouldn't be gone long. In his slumber he didn't hear her words. She spoke more to reassure herself than anything else. Gathering up her weapons she ventured down the bank towards the ocean. Nearer to the water the grassland would be softer than the dense beach where Ryu now slept. She could fashion a poultice from banana leaves and mud.

Without a sheath for Bhrytbyrn she had to drag the massive blade behind her. Carrying the whip of bones upon her hip chafed her wound so she wrapped that around her torso instead. She must've looked a strange sight shuffling across the beach in disarray.

At the water's edge she sat upon her knees and tried to flush her wound. The saltwater stung each time it pooled over the cut causing Rayna to wince. She only hoped it was enough to keep infection from taking hold.

The wet sand proved too loose to keep its shape upon her side. What she needed was dark mud and thick leaves. That meant she would have to move further inland. Rayna looked back towards where Ryu slept. She wondered if he could stream a small enough flame to cauterize her wound. Those straying thoughts led her down a nightmarish scene of going up like a torch.

Ryu was still just a young dragon. She didn't know how much control he held over his fire breath. It didn't make sense to chance it. Still, she hated wandering so far away from him. She just got Ryu back from the dragon witch Nadiuska. If she lost him again, she would go mad.

But the parting gift Nadiuska left at Rayna's side was starting to ache up into her ribs. She could feel the cold trickle of blood oozing out down her skin. It began to pool in the creases of her armor which grew heavier with each step she took.

Rayna thought about stripping the armor and burying

it in the sand. But she couldn't bring herself to part with it. Suppose someone happened to stumble across it and they made off with the lot? The armor was high quality and would certainly fetch a fair price at market. But it meant more to Rayna than all that.

The man it belonged to once saved her life and lost his in the process. Wearing his armor as she headed into battle made her feel as though she honored Valerios in some small way. So, she trudged on relying upon the strength of her body to maintain the weight of the armor.

A man she knew on the land of Kartha had also saved her once. Those days seemed so long ago but with each step Rayna took she saw his face clearer in her mind.

Toth was born on Kartha and carried the darker complexion like the others kissed by their island sun. He was tall, much taller than Rayna herself, with a lean musculature built from adventure seeking. Toth could never sit still for too long without racing off to swim in the deep waters or climb the highest peak.

Rayna scarcely remembered his long, wavy hair not slick with water or perspiration. He thirsted for life and enjoyed challenging himself. One of those challenges he aimed to conquer had been Rayna herself. And once Toth set his mind to something he usually accomplished it.

She was taken with him at first sight as most women were. He was like a Source God in the form of a man.

But Rayna would make Toth work for her affection which created a deeper bond than any single night of passion would've.

Rayna recalled how their days at play would last for hours. Whether they were fishing, fucking, or hunting it made them lose all sense of time until Toth's brother had to come looking and brought them back. Even now Rayna heard the gallop of horses as she thought back on her past in Kartha. Another step deeper into the brambles of a fallen forest and she realized the sound of hooves were not in her head. They were very real and growing very close.

She'd traveled far from the beach coming upon what she thought would be a lush tropical forest. Inside she expected to source what she needed for her wound including fresh water and food. On closer inspection she found it had succumbed to the elements of wildfire. No shred of thick, billowing trees remained making it impossible to hide from the approaching riders.

Though wounded and weary, Rayna stood her ground. She hefted her sword up in both hands and awaited the inevitable fight. If she fell, she hoped Ryu would get away safely. Guarding the dragon had become her life's work. She wasn't going to stop now, not even for the King of Kartha.

2
Spirit Watchers

Though wounded and weary, Rayna stood her ground. She hefted her sword up in both hands and awaited the inevitable fight. If she fell, she hoped Ryu would get away safely. Guarding the dragon had become her life's work. She wasn't going to stop now, not even for the King of Kartha.

The riders came hard and fast. Before Rayna could discern which direction they approached from, she was surrounded. Ten riders in all circled her from every side. She kept on a swivel trying desperately to mark an escape path.

Every riding brigade had one weak link like a faulty piece of chain mail. Rayna knew how to expose that weakness to her benefit. Only this time she wouldn't find a weak rider within the pack. The contrast of bright red against white marked their faces in streaks of paint.

These were the colors of the king's army known as the Spirit Watchers. Red for the God of Fire who legend claimed lived beneath Kartha; white representing precious shells from a sacred part of the island.

Their thick, layered leather armor was molded to each rider to protect the wearer without inhibiting movement. Only the leader wore metal plate armor over his leathers. Resources were scarce on Kartha but they more than made up for it with their skill.

The Spirit Watchers were wardens of the land who upheld the rule put forth by the reigning king. Unlike on Atharia where votes and violence chose their leaders, Kartha knew only one clan who sat upon their throne. Bronze skinned, dark-haired, and protective of their land. Any outsider to Kartha was easily spotted and either killed on sight or brought to the king for questioning.

Now that Rayna knew who she was dealing with it became unwise to continue aggressively. Wounded, tired, and outnumbered the pack would cut her down without effort. Instead of her usual tactics she opted for trying diplomacy and lowered her sword.

"I am not your enemy," she told them. "Let me speak with King Krato. He'll vouch for me."

The Watchers looked at each other with concern and confusion. They spoke in a foreign tongue Rayna had long since forgotten. She only picked up clicks of the conversation and it didn't bode well for her. The

Watchers called her mad or misinformed, she couldn't discern which but neither sounded good.

Rayna watched closely as the circle of horses tightened on her. If she must fight to survive, she would do so with honor. Fortunately, it didn't come to that. The leader pushed his horse forwards and looked down upon Rayna a moment before issuing her his hand.

"Come." He spoke in her native tongue as he reached out.

Rayna saw no other way out of her predicament. Though she didn't want to go with the Spirit Watchers and leave Ryu behind it was the only option at the moment. She accepted the leader's hand as he helped her up into the saddle behind him.

They let her keep hold of Bhrytbyrn. The Watcher wasn't concerned of a sneak attack from a lone, wounded warrior. A quick turn into formation and they headed out of the fallen forest. As they passed through Laihaka Valley, Rayna could only assume the Watchers meant to take her to the City of Tanoa'i. There the King of Kartha would await. She didn't really know if he would accept her back after what happened with his son. But Rayna saw no other way out of this mess.

~

Riding across the valley, clinging to the sweat covered back of the leader, Rayna noted the destruction that had fallen over the island. The last time she traveled through Kartha it flourished with lush tropical plants. Now, every bit appeared to be burned under a heavy flame.

Laihaka Valley used to open into a paradise of colors blooming across it. Rayna always felt like she was in a dream running through the tall grass surrounded by majestic floral patterns. But few remained standing in the valley. Only pockets of colors were visible among a dull backdrop of ash.

"What happened here?" She couldn't help but ask.

Again came the Karithik language falling foreign on her ears. All she could decipher this time was the word "fire." That seemed obvious given the destruction to the land Rayna witnessed so far. Then the Watcher spoke again, this time using the phrase "from the air."

A lump caught in Rayna's throat. Fire from the air could only mean one thing: a dragon. She knew it hadn't been Ryu but if a dragon had decimated their island, and they found Rayna traveling with one, it would be both their heads. The Spirit Watchers didn't waste time on ceremony, but they did enjoy spectacle.

Rayna would be buried to the neck, her head poking out of the sand awaiting the end. They would take turns, and it would be slow, but eventually they would take turns riding over her with the horses until they trampled her to death.

She'd seen such punishment before when visiting

Kartha. The thought of such a gruesome end made her shiver. It caused the Watcher to push her away from him and she almost fell from the horse. She stabilized herself for a moment, but the jerking of the horse exacerbated her wound.

Each gallop felt like a thousand knives to her side. Rayna's body had taken its share of abuse throughout her years of dragon hunting. She had the scars and even a missing eye to prove it. But the damage this time hurt more than any she could remember. Without treatment for so long she was starting to feel weak with blood loss.

When the group rounded the hillside towards Tanoa'i, their historic city by the sea, Rayna couldn't hold on any longer. Inches from the gates to Krato Castle she fell from the horse. The sand felt much denser than she remembered as her face and torso crashed down into it.

The Spirit Watchers reacted as though Rayna tried to escape them. They surrounded her with their horses while two of the men jumped down and grabbed her arms and legs. She didn't struggle against their grips; she couldn't. Her head lolled back and forth as they dragged her the rest of the way inside. All she saw before blacking out was a dark shape traveling across the sky.

3
Fever

Rayna came in and out of consciousness several times. Each time her surroundings were different. The interior of a hut; a bath house; a stylish bed chamber. She couldn't stay awake long enough to understand where they'd taken her. A few times it felt as though they were torturing her as heat and needles came to her side. After that, she lost consciousness completely.

When she fully woke it felt as though she'd been tied down to a bed. Rayna panicked and struggled against her bonds. Only there were no ropes or chains holding her against her will. Her own body held her down. Every limb felt so heavy with aching she could barely move.

With significant effort she managed to pull herself into a sitting position. Any movement caused her to perspire. Once she sat up the wound at her side stung in such a way that it made her cry out. Her hand went to it expecting to touch blood. Instead, she found it had been bandaged with great care. This was more than the simple poultice she intended on making. Her wounds had been stitched and covered with strips of plant fibers soaked in vinegar.

Shaking off the fatigue and disorientation of waking, Rayna found herself not in a dungeon but a villa of sorts. The structure was built of thick bamboo with a thatched roof of palm leaves. She lay on a bed of the finest silks with plump, goose feather pillows. Adjacent from the bed an open window provided an unobstructed view of the sea.

Across that vast ocean stood her homeland of Atharia. As pleasant as the surroundings appeared to be Rayna wanted to gather her dragon and go home. Struggling to move again she swung her lungs over the bed and tried to stand. Her first steps felt as though she were a babe learning to walk again. She took a tumble into a table set up near the bed. The edge of it bumped her wound causing her to shriek.

A commotion erupted outside, and Rayna heard feet rushing towards the door. She looked around the room for Bhrytbyrn and couldn't find her sword. A nearby chair made of heavy, dark wood acted as her weapon. But when she tried to heft it, she could only bring it waist high. The strength had left her body and she felt weak as a child.

Still, she would fight with everything she had when the person or persons made their way through the door. As it cracked open a woman poked her head in and gasped as she saw Rayna standing there. Only momentarily startled the woman came into the room and started lecturing Rayna to get back in bed.

She was a small woman with many years lining her sun kissed skin. Though Rayna was twice her size the woman wouldn't back down. Speaking mostly in Karithik and hand gestures she instructed Rayna to lay on the bed.

The words "ill" and "need rest" came through clearly enough that Rayna obliged the woman. She settled back on the bed as the older lady pressed her palm to Rayna's forehead. Her nose crinkled up with concern and she shouted for others at the door. Rayna flinched as more people came their way. The woman sensed her distress and tried to calm her by soothing back her hair.

"Please, tell me where I am," Rayna said, her voice hoarse with dehydration.

No reply came from the woman but when another joined them in the room they began chattering like birds. This one was younger yet dressed in the same peculiar garb of white linens with a head shroud to match. She carried a tray set with stripped coconut, fresh plant fiber wraps, and a folded, wet towel.

The older one took the coconut and brought it to Rayna's mouth. She hesitated at first but after a few sips of the sweet nectar she tried to drink the entire fruit. The woman took it from her before that happened.

"Not too much," she said in Rayna's traditional tongue. "Bad for bowel."

Rayna nodded though she wanted more. The cool liquid on her tongue felt refreshing and helped her regain some vigor. The two women continued to aide Rayna by re-wrapping her wound and setting the cold compress to her head.

"Fever," the young one said. "This will help."

Seeing that they meant her no harm, and too weak to argue, Rayna let them care for her. Before too long she fell back to sleep. When she woke again sometime later it was dark outside. She could hear the waves gently beating against the shore like a rhythmic chant.

This time she managed to stand without falling. She felt some strength return to her body though not all of it. The table and chair had been set back up in the corner of the room. A dazzling array of fruit and bread rested on a tray there beckoning Rayna's hungry belly.

If it were a deception, she was too famished to care. Besides, why would the women care for her wounds only to poison her after? Rayna scuttled towards the table on shaking legs. She collapsed into the chair and then fell on the food like a rabid animal.

Everything tasted fresh from the island. Only Kartha carried such magnificent, exotic fruits. Each bite was succulent and juicy, the bread crisp on the outside and still warm in the middle. A pitcher of water came with the meal and Rayna drank down about half of it before she began to feel stuffed.

Belly full and fever broken, she leaned back in her chair and tried to assess the situation. The only way she could get solid answers was to try and remember the Karithik language. Eyes closed she thought back to her lessons with Toth. He had been sweet and gentle with his instruction. Each time Rayna got a word right he would kiss her. Eventually they abandoned the lesson and instead spoke the universal language of love making. Rayna had become very adept at that skill though it wouldn't help her predicament now.

She would have to make do with the broken fragmentation of the language and hope the women would understand. Forcing herself to stand she went to the door. Taking a deep breath she turned the handle. It was unlocked; she wasn't a prisoner. A good sign but Rayna still wanted to leave. Ryu must've woken by now and become anxious that she wasn't with him. She needed to get back.

4
Sword of Sight

Fully clothed in a white dressing gown, Rayna still felt exposed. She wanted her armor and her weapons. By the Source Gods where was her eyepatch? If the women caring for her saw the state of her missing eye, they didn't make mention of it. Or perhaps they had, and Rayna couldn't understand the language.

She picked up speed trying to navigate her way through a maze of huts. Each of them looked like the other. In her weakened condition Rayna wound up getting confused and turned around several times.

Finally, she stumbled upon a path of stones she hadn't noticed before in the dark. They led her to a crossroads that broke off in three different directions. One went downhill; one uphill; and the other continued towards the beach. Never mind the dialogue with the women when escape was clear. She started towards the beach intent on following it back towards the hilltop where Ryu would be waiting. But a nagging in her gut caused her to turn around.

Rayna needed Bhrytbyrn. There was too much history wrapped up in that exquisitely crafted sword including her own eye resting in the hilt. In her earlier years, the bejeweled dragon eye caused her much grief. A curse from the witch Nadiuska, she used it to guide Rayna like a puppet, slaughtering every dragon on Atharia out of a misplaced grudge. Eventually the witch took the eye back from Rayna by ripping it from her head and then placing it upon the sword.

Regardless of past pain she felt, the eye, like the sword itself, were parts of Rayna's essence. She had defeated the witch and laid to rest a torment that dominated most of her life. That didn't mean Rayna wanted to start over and become someone new. Settling down as a wife and a mother didn't appeal to her. The only child she wanted to care for was the dragon child.

Ryu already outgrew her, but he was still innocent. To protect him from those that would cause him harm she needed her sword. Somewhere back in one of those huts Bhrytbyrn waited for her to come and claim it.

Rayna would need to stay quiet in her search, so no alarms were raised. She expected that the Spirit Watchers did not go far. They must've brought her to the medicine women for care. If they caught her walking around, they would no doubt set her in chains.

Staggering back down the path of stones with bare feet made her long for her boots as well. Each step was jarring as though her hips sat off kilter. A few feet more and she returned to the grouping of huts. The sensible course of action would be to search hers first. Perhaps they put the sword and her clothing out of sight. Rayna hadn't had time to do a thorough search before.

Stepping back through the door she was caught by surprise. Spirit Watchers swarmed the room. They shouted in Karithik at the sight of her and dragged her inside. Rayna tried her best to fight back and for that she was subdued with chains just as she expected.

The medicine women came and tried to argue on her behalf. Rayna picked up fragments that said she was too ill to be handled in such a rough manner. The Spirit Watchers didn't care. Their concern was the safety of those that resided on Kartha. Rayna was a foreigner to their land and therefore a threat to their way of life.

They took her from the safety of the small huts, and the care of the kind women, and forced her on horseback once more. This time they bound her hands to the horn of the saddle. Their horses were well-trained, and this one followed the rest of the pack as instructed. Rayna could kick and make commands all she wanted but the horse would not listen.

Her body began to ache once again as the horse trotted up a path with the others. Given her weakened condition, Rayna was at their mercy. But once she regained full strength there would be retribution for whatever torture they meant to put her through.

5
Krato Castle

It wasn't long before they returned to the gates of Krato Castle. The makeshift medical refuge sat just down on the hillside. In the dark with her head dizzy from fever she couldn't discern the City of Tanoa'i.

It was different than Rayna remembered. Before the city was thriving with merchants and magic dealers. Anything a person could want would be found in Tanoa'i due to their trades with Valeuki on Atharia. Now everything seemed diminished just like the charred remnants of Laihaka Valley.

Had Rayna made her way north at the crossroads rather than turning back she would've reached the castle on her own. Now she was brought in chains. Not a very fitting homecoming for one who almost became the princess of Kartha.

This lot would not remember her from those days. The

job of the Spirit Watcher was to patrol the island. They didn't venture inland unless it were important—like a muscular, blonde foreigner threatening their safety. But Rayna would never forget those months she spent on Kartha. Her time alongside Toth is one of the main reasons she refused to open her heart to anyone ever again.

Now wrought with emotional pain alongside the physical, Rayna wanted nothing more than to rest. They could throw her in a dank cell with no windows and it wouldn't matter so long as she could lay down. But she wasn't taken to the cells. Instead, the Spirit Watchers pulled her from the horse and handed her off to the castle guards. Then they went on their way.

The guards, a male and a female, were both dressed in dark leathers from head-to-toe. Their faces remained free of paint except for a small Karithik symbol resting under the right eye. It signified the rule of the throne and their loyalty to it.

Apparently, Rayna was now the problem of the Royal Watchers. They were an angry lot, duty-bound to the strict rules of the kingdom. It was one of the reasons Toth rebelled so much. He was the heir to the throne but held no interest in that claim. It was one of the reasons Rayna fell in love with him back then. She never held any use for royalty either. After the mess she left back on Atharia, she would've preferred not to see a king or queen ever again.

Now the royal house of King Krato held her. If he were in a good mood, and slightly drunk, he would pardon her, and Rayna could be on her way. But if Krato still held a grudge from her past actions, then Rayna's life may be in danger.

The Royal Watchers marched her through the back entry of the castle so as not to arouse concern. It was early with the sun just now peeking its head up from slumber. The castle staff would be awakening as well. The Royal Watchers didn't want a panic to erupt as they paraded their fair-skinned prisoner around.

Rayna didn't recognize anything from before. It seemed Krato Castle was no longer a lavish spectacle. Instead, the interior felt more subdued and simplistic. The open floor plan saw the kitchens and the dining area come together as one. A glimpse across the room and Rayna could see where the king himself sat. His throne no longer the design of iron workers. Instead, a combination of palm fronds and thick bamboo came together to make the royal chair.

She couldn't help but smile in spite of her predicament. As the Royal Watchers marched her along, she noted it was a much more welcoming environment. Very different from the cold, hard rule of Saltwood Stronghold back on Atharia. Or the damp and dark Majestic Mountains where Queen Nadiuska's stronghold once stood.

The way Krato Castle was designed now is exactly what Toth always dreamed of. No overbearing ruler separating classes of people in a hierarchy. Instead, all came together for the betterment of the island. Rayna didn't know why the changes were made, or what befell the island of Kartha, but she was certain it wasn't because of Toth.

When her legs began to grow weary the Royal Watchers dragged her the rest of the way. This included going up a long set of wooden steps. Though Rayna felt diminished and undernourished the mass of her muscle still caused a problem for the female guard. She struggled to hold Rayna up high enough as they walked. This caused the edge of the steps to catch her in the shins and knees several times.

At the top of the stairs, it split into living quarters. These rooms were separated from each other by large wooden doors. The King of Kartha would have his own room at the opposite end of the castle. At least, that's how it used to be. With the new arrangement the Royal Watchers could be taking Rayna to him right now.

They did not. Rather, she was brought to a private chamber where the guards unchained her hands and released her. Rayna grew wary as the female stepped out while the male guard kept watch over her. He stood with arms folded blocking the door. Rayna stepped back and surveyed the room while keeping a close eye on the man. Should he advance, she would make good use of her teeth as a weapon and tear out his jugular like an animal.

The room was modest with a small bed, a simple dining setup, and a bathing tub. Rayna's eyes fixated on the tub longing to feel the warm water caress her bruised body. She turned back to the Royal Watcher and tried her best to converse with him.

"Why am I here?" she asked.

He tilted his head, confused by her language. She tried again in broken Karithik but still failed to get her point across. After fumbling over her words and getting nowhere the female guard returned with fresh clothing and linens. She set them down on the bed then motioned to Rayna.

"Bathe, dress," she said.

After giving the orders, the Royal Watchers stepped out of the room. Rayna tried to stop the female by catching her arm. She desperately wanted some answers, and it seemed as though the girl understood some of her language. But touching the guard was a mistake. She at once went on the defensive and pushed Rayna back with force. Then the male interceded with his own shove. This knocked Rayna to the ground and caused her wounded side to flare up in pain.

The Royal Watchers looked down on her with a mix of aggression and concern. But the concern wasn't for

Rayna. She discerned from their countenances that they weren't supposed to harm her in any way. Orders from the king perhaps or the medicine women from before? They argued with each other and then the girl once again laid out commands for Rayna.

"Bathe, dress, rest."

At that, the two of them left the room, locking the door behind them. It wasn't a cell, but Rayna was still a prisoner in Krato Castle. She grew tired of being dragged across Kartha. Ryu must be frantic by now that she hadn't returned to him.

Though her mind and spirit wanted to break free her body couldn't be convinced. So, she did as the guards asked and slipped into the warm bath. The water was filled with healing salts that soothed her weary bones. It relaxed Rayna so well she almost fell asleep right there in the bath.

They left her a new cotton dressing gown. She didn't bother with it. Instead, she dried off and chose to sleep in the nude. Her naked body exposed to the island air always gave her a sense of peace. As she lay on the bed, she imagined Toth next to her. She could almost feel the warmth of his skin and the pulse of his heartbeat.

Remembering their time together almost caused her mind and hand to stray. Her fingertips were inches from pleasuring herself when a knock on the door reminded Rayna she wasn't in a safe space. Rolling from the bed, she pulled on the gown then tried her best to reply.

"It's locked. I can't let you in."

The handle turned and the door opened. To Rayna's surprise it was not a guard or a servant standing there. At first, she thought Toth stood before her. The man in the doorway shared the same dark eyes and thick hair as her former lover. But she knew it couldn't be him. Toth was dead.

6
King of Kartha

My dear, Rayna. It is you after all."

He looked like Toth and spoke like him as well. The two of them always shared similarities but Talakai was much younger than his brother in those days. He often tried to tag along whenever Toth and Rayna tried to slip off on their own. If Toth didn't let him join them on their adventures, Talakai would tell their father. He was a bit of a brat in those days.

Looking at him now, Rayna saw a capable, strong warrior standing before her. But more than that, she could tell by the drape of his clothes, and the crown of thorns upon his head, that Talakai was the new King of Kartha.

"The Spirit Watchers sent word they caught an intruder to our lands," Talakai continued, speaking perfectly in her native tongue. "When they gave the description, I knew it couldn't be anyone else but you."

He reached his hand out to caress her cheek and it caused Rayna to lurch back. She had no intention of being disrespectful, but Talakai reminded her of Toth a little too much. He grew agitated at her reaction and balled his hand into a fist. Apparently, the same temper ran through their bloodline.

"What they didn't tell me is why you're back on Kartha after all this time."

"A mistake, Talakai," she confessed. "I traveled here by accident. You must believe that I never meant to return here."

"But I don't believe you, Rayna," he said calmly. "I don't believe it was an accident at all. Fate brought you here."

"Fate?"

"Destiny, fate, whatever you want to call it," he explained. "You were meant to come back. Kartha needs you."

Rayna couldn't help but scoff. "There's no use for a fair-skinned woman on your shores. The last time I was here your father reminded me of that daily. Where is he anyway? I should like to ask his permission to leave."

"My father died a long time ago," Talakai told her. "With what happened to Toth that left me to take the throne. And unfortunately, I cannot grant you leave just yet."

Rayna felt overwhelmed. She sat back towards the edge of the bed and almost missed it entirely. Talakai had to catch her under the arm before she fell to the ground. He helped her to sit and then lingered a little too long and a little too close.

Rayna kept his stare as he studied her face. Even with a horrible burn scar where her left eye used to be, Talakai didn't draw away in disgust. He excused himself out of respect for her personal space and stepped back.

"I'm sorry to hear of your father," Rayna said softly. "I assumed you'd taken the throne, but it didn't dawn on me that he'd passed. My head is still a bit fuzzy."

"You had a terrible fever from an infected wound. Aga and Linae did what they could to help. They said you might feel weak for a few days as the infection fades. They also suggested that you rest."

He stepped over to her table and poured water from a clay pitcher. Wiping the spill from the side of the cup against his royal tunic he offered it to her. She thanked him and drank slowly letting the water coat her tongue and the roof of her mouth before swallowing.

"The sisters are trained healers. So, you should heed their advice. But you look strong to me," Talakai told her with a smile.

"I look like a wreck. I've been through many battles the last of which brought me to Kartha by accident not fate."

"I disagree on all counts." He reached out his hand to her. "Come, I've had a sumptuous meal prepared. I'm sure you're famished."

Rayna squeezed his hand then pulled away. "I'll take it in here, thank you."

"Nonsense." Talakai took her under the arm and insisted she stand. "You'll dine with me. I wish to hear of all your exploits."

She knew better than to argue then. Talakai wanted something from her. It was the same reason the guards refused to let her leave. Trouble had come to paradise and the young King of Kartha got it into his head that Rayna was their savior.

7
Wine, Dine, & Dragons

Unlike the roughshod way the Royal Watchers dragged her through the castle, Talakai led her with grace. He held her by the hand and kept her close to him as they walked. Either he feared she may fall again, or he didn't want her trying to run.

By now Rayna knew better. She would play along until she found a more opportune moment to retrieve her belongings and get back to her dragon. Still, she couldn't help being intrigued by all of this. As much as it pained her to be away from Ryu for so long, Rayna also wanted to hear of Talakai's exploits. What had happened on Kartha since she'd been away?

He took her to the dining area, and it instantly reminded her of a time in her past. When Rayna was very young, she fell in with a mercenary group called the Forsaken Force. Led by Darius the Dreaded, a formidable thief and swordsman, the rowdy lot of young men welcomed Rayna as one of their own.

In Darius' compound they always ate together as a family. That's what Rayna saw now. A cluster of people all come together for the morning meal inside Krato Castle. Their king would eat with them and Rayna as his guest. But first, Talakai offered her up to the crowd like a deity.

"I need everyone to stop what they're doing and listen."

The people halted in their gathering of food and chatter. They turned their full attention to Talakai as he marched with Rayna to the front of the dining hall. There they stood facing the groupings of tables and the people staring back at them.

Rayna couldn't help but feel exposed as she stood in nothing but a thin dressing gown that hugged her curves. More than that, she didn't have her eyepatch. The entire community of Tanoa'i seemed to be there observing her. A foreign devil to their lands that Talakai was presenting like his queen.

He spoke to his constituents in their native Karithik. Many times, Rayna heard her name, but the rest of their words were lost on her ears. She wanted to pull her hand from his, cover her missing eye, and run down to the beach. Then she smelled the food and her stomach had other ideas.

How long had it been since she had a full, hot meal?

The aroma of roasted pig and sweet corn made her salivate. It brought up a sense memory for her of a time when Toth brought her home to meet his father. They enjoyed their roasted pig in Krato Castle. But the king didn't enjoy meeting Rayna. He wasn't impressed with the young girl who claimed to be a dragonslayer. Her exploits on Atharia had not yet reached their shores and King Krato called her a liar.

Now it seemed her legend had grown so large it came across the ocean to all of Tanoa'i. At the conclusion of Talakai's speech the people stood and applauded Rayna. Talakai raised her arm in the air and then gave his own applause.

Rayna wasn't much for fanfare. Even across Atharia when she was recognized as the slayer of mighty dragons, she tried to downplay it. Someone always wanted to test the slayer. She didn't go looking for trouble, but it found her anyway. Now her troubles came in an unfamiliar language. The one-word Rayna made out made her more nervous than a thousand blades pointed at her breast.

Talakai called her "champion." The ramifications of such an honor were overwhelming. Rayna tried to stop him, to talk him down from such delusions. But the Tanoa'i people began to cry out the word as well. They chanted it from their dining tables, from the kitchens, and all around.

Their collective voices thundered through the castle erupting in waves of energy that came crashing back over Rayna. The immense weight of such a burden felt heavier than a full-grown dragon's foot on her back. She tried to quiet them, but her gestures only caused them to grow louder. Finally, she tugged on the sleeve of Talakai's tunic and whispered to him.

"Please, make them stop."

"Why? They honor you."

"How could they honor me after what I did to their prince?"

The memory stung as she spoke it and she felt the sudden burst of tears fill her remaining eye. Frustrated with her show of emotion she turned her head. Talakai took her under the chin and turned her to face him again.

"You are not responsible for what happened to Toth," he told her. "I'm sorry that you carried that guilt with you all this time. And I'm aware of the weight of this burden I'm setting on your shoulders now. But you're the only one who can help us restore Kartha to its former glory."

"You called me your champion."

He smiled. "You are."

Talakai put up his hand to quiet the people. Then he gave them leave to continue eating. He and Rayna sat at the front of the room and dined at the king's table. Food was brought to them in several courses. Rayna tried to mind her manners and not eat like a savage. But when the succulent pork came to them, she couldn't pretend anymore. Her last full meal had been days before leaving Atharia.

Since then, the situation and her fever precluded her from being able to dine without it upsetting her stomach. Now, with the tantalizing aroma of roast pig under her nose she found her appetite again.

Talakai had been using cutlery to eat his meals to that point. When he saw Rayna fall on the food with her bare hands, he had a laugh then joined her. She would've felt embarrassment if the pangs of hunger weren't so fierce.

"You always did things your own way," he told her.

Rayna wiped her chin of juices, took a swig of wine and a deep breath, then addressed the topic Talakai seemed to be avoiding. Now that she was starting to get her energy back it was time to discover what exactly Talakai wanted from her. She started with a question that had been nagging at her since entering Krato Castle.

"Speaking of doing things your way, I see you've changed how your father ran his court."

"I'd like to say it was by design, but it was more of a necessity than a brilliant, strategic move on my part." He admitted. "We had to condense everything. It's no longer safe to be spread across the island. When the castle was rebuilt, that's when it became the vision you see now."

Rayna looked around the room with confusion and surprise. Only now when she wasn't being dragged by guards did she realize the entire castle structure had changed. If the original Krato Castle fell, she was beginning to put the pieces together on their need for her services. It seemed Kartha was under attack.

"This is not the same castle then?" She sought confirmation of her suspicions.

"You have been away a long time," Talakai chuckled. "Krato Castle once stood on the other side of the island. Now it is forbidden to go there."

He joked but there was pain behind his eyes that made Rayna reach out to him. She set her hand upon his arm and gave it a light squeeze. The gesture made him uneasy. He patted her hand and then pulled his arm away to pour more wine from the pitcher in front of them. It was refreshing to see a king care for himself rather than call a servant for everything little action.

"Talakai, what's happened here?" Rayna asked with genuine concern. "The land has been charred, Krato Castle is gone, and your father...well, I never would've guessed to see the day where he gave up his throne. He always used to tell me that his ghost would still be wandering around the grounds after he passed on."

"You believe in spirits then?"

"It was said in jest to lighten the mood," she admitted. "My apologies."

"No, you're right. My father used to say that often. He'd also boast how they'd have to pry his sword from his cold, dead fingers. We buried him with it out back in the gardens. As for his spirit, it may well be wandering the lands. The Spirit Watchers have yet to spot it though."

"You don't have to talk about it," Rayna told him. "I shouldn't have brought it up."

Talakai shook his head. "No, you want to know what happened on Kartha. I'll tell you."

He pushed the meal to the side and stood offering his hand to her. She accepted and the two of them walked from the dining hall. No doubt Talakai wanted to keep their discussion away from his constituents. The less they knew about the truth the better.

Should a panic set in Talakai wouldn't be able to control them. Rayna sensed a firm hand but not an experienced ruler on the throne. His brother was the one being groomed to take over. Talakai was thrust into that position after Toth's early demise and the fall of King Krato.

As they walked Rayna marked a handful of Royal Watchers at their flank and their sides. They guarded their king but not from Rayna. Something else plagued their land. Whatever it was had taken the life of his father and she sensed Talakai feared it would come for him next.

"There have been strange happenings on the island for some time now," Talakai admitted.

They walked with arms linked together upon a garden path. Rayna grew concerned Talakai would bring her to see his father's grave marker. She'd already witnessed too much death in her young life. Better to remember Krato as the jovial man he used to be.

"For a long while we felt rumblings beneath our feet," Talakai continued. "Strange sounds came from our forests. Even the animals seemed spooked about something. My father commissioned scholars to discover the origins of these occurrences. They told him it may be volcanic activity. At one time it lay dormant beneath our lands, but an unknown entity triggered it."

They moved slowly around the castle grounds not seeking any specific location. This was not a tour, rather a simple stroll under the morning sky. Talakai wove his tale of destruction while enjoying what beauty remained on their land.

Rayna basked in it as well. Settled and no longer on the run, she was able to appreciate the surroundings and community. The entire city of Tanoa'i worked together to make their home not only formidable but warm and inviting.

"My father grew skeptical about the scholars' assessment," Talakai said. "He sent warriors out to find the so-called volcano only they never returned."

Rayna involuntarily flinched at his words. Her arm squeezed Talakai's and then she pulled away. He stopped walking and stared at her with concern. A quick smile and a fast-thought lie assuaged him.

"I felt dizzy for a moment," she said. "I'm better now."

She took his arm again and they continued to walk with the guards still flanking them on all sides. Rayna wasn't about to admit what she'd really felt at that moment. The last time a king told her his best guards had gone missing on a mission those guards had been burned alive by a dragon.

It had been Ryu's mother who charred the best of the Saltwood Soldiers on Atharia. But Rayna had inadvertently killed her. In fact, she killed most of the dragons across Atharia. Only two escaped that fate: Ryu and the massive male dragon Nazalon.

Rayna's interaction with Nazalon came during her transition from dragon slayer to dragon protector. He told her to watch over Ryu and keep him safe from the clutches of the witch Nadiuska. Then Nazalon left Atharia. Had he come to Kartha and wreaked havoc on the people there?

Rayna kept quiet and listened to Talakai's story trying to pick up any details that said a dragon threatened their land. If it meant getting back to Ryu and away from Kartha, Rayna may need to slay one more dragon.

8

What Lies Beneath

When they grew weary of walking Talakai brought her to a secluded spot underneath a large banyan tree. A bench of wood and twine had been set up next to a marker of sorts. As they walked closer Rayna noted it as a memorial stone. Talakai took her to his father's grave after all.

"Krato?" she asked, motioning towards the stone.

Talakai shook his head. "No, Toth actually."

The mention of his name in correlation to the death stone made Rayna shudder. Talakai mistook her discomfort for a chill. He removed his own tunic and wrapped it around her shoulders.

It felt soft against her skin but smelled of his musk. The scent of him reminded her of Toth. As did the look of his muscular build now exposed through a linen chemise.

Rayna hugged the tunic to her shoulders letting the intricately woven fibers caress her skin. She sat on the bench and stared out at the stone marker. Letting her thoughts wander to days gone by, she absently addressed the loss out loud.

"Do you ever miss him?"

Talakai sat next to her. "Sometimes. But you know as well as I that Toth was a handful."

"He was your brother."

"Yes. But he was still an ass."

Rayna turned to him. Still conscious of her disfigured eye being exposed she looked away again. Her focus fell again to the stone as she tried to issue an apology.

"I'm sorry for what happened to him. In all fairness you should've taken my head by now."

"I don't want your head, Rayna. I keep telling you I need your sword."

At that, he motioned to his guards. One of them stepped forward and handed over a large satchel. Talakai took it then ordered him back. He fished around in the sack and then revealed the contents to Rayna. It was Bhrytbyrn, her massive broadsword, polished with a fresh leather wrap on the hilt.

She wanted to snatch the blade from him but envisioned the guards tackling her to the ground. Instead, she forced herself to remain calm and allow Talakai to present the sword to her. He wanted a grand showing as though it were an extension of peace between them. Rayna didn't know how deep that peace could actually go given her history with this family. But she would gladly accept the sword back in her possession.

The familiar heft in her hands gave her renewed vigor. She wanted to test out her strength with a few overhead swings but continued to stay patient. In time, she'd be at full strength, saddled on the back of Ryu, and headed for home. For now, she remained at Talakai's whims.

"Is that your eye?" he asked, his voice trembling in disbelief as he tapped the jewel in the hilt.

Rayna acknowledged the question with a nod. Before he continued his prodding, she gave him the full story. It was bound to come up eventually. Better to get it all out and move on.

"Turns out a powerful witch cursed me with that jeweled dragon eye," Rayna explained. "Unbeknownst to me at the time it connected the two of us. Her influence helped me to track and kill dragons under the guise of foul lie. Once I broke that pact, she wanted her prize returned to her. So, she ripped the jewel from my skull before cauterizing my flesh with magic fire. Then she stuck it on the sword to continue using the power of the dragon eye."

The full story didn't seem to jar Talakai until she mentioned "magic fire." He was no good at covering his tell signs and Rayna marked them easily. Something in those words made him uncomfortable. Rayna would need to find a way to draw out his secrets. For now, she had a simple request.

"If you could fashion me an eye patch, I would very much like to cover up the scar from that encounter," she told him.

Another word to his guards and they produced a silken cloth. Talakai gently wrapped it around Rayna's head then smoothed it down with his fingers. The delicate way in which he touched her sparked a new concern. Talakai had always been enamored with her as a boy. It seemed the man still harbored strong feelings that she didn't return.

"We don't discriminate on these lands but if it makes you feel better, I'll have a proper patch sewn for you." he said. "Until then, the silk will have to be enough."

With the understanding of her reason for being at the castle changed, Rayna grew more brazen. Talakai wasn't going to throw her in a cell or inflict torture. He needed her, for what he still hadn't said. But knowing that he cared for her meant Rayna could push certain issues without fear of retribution.

"What about my armor?"

"The sword isn't enough?"

"It's a package deal."

"All in good time, Rayna." He patted her hand. "You'll

get your armor, a horse, even that hideous whip made of human spines you traveled here with. All you need to do is agree to be my champion."

Rayna's grip tightened on Bhrytbyrn's hilt. She was tired of the games. "What does that mean?"

"The troubles on Kartha started when you left here," Talakai began. "They intensified recently as though a shift fell across the entire world. Then you returned with tales of battling a powerful witch...one of the oldest instances of Source Magic."

He stood and paced in front of her with his hands folded at his back. Rayna began to tense up. The mood shifted and she faulted her earlier assessment. Perhaps he wasn't as forgiving as she thought.

"I know you still see that young, foolish boy before you," Talakai said. "But I'm a king now and I am no fool."

He stopped pacing and turned to face her. Standing over her while she sat gave him some sense of power. She let him revel in it knowing in her heart that if she wanted it the lot of them would be dead within seconds. Now that she held her sword again nothing would stand in her way. Except maybe Talakai's request.

"Whatever you did on Atharia disrupted the entire world. We felt it all the way over here and it decimated our once lavish land."

Rayna started to argue her own point when Talakai

silenced her. The guards set their hands on her shoulders to make certain she stayed seated while he finished speaking.

"I need you to fix it, Rayna," Talakai went on. "I'll provide you with whatever you require but you're not leaving Kartha until things are made right."

Finally, it was Rayna's turn to speak. She wouldn't hold back. Voice raised with concern and confusion she lashed out. Guards or king mattered not.

"Fix what, Talakai? What torment befell Kartha that I could be responsible for?"

Talakai laughed as though the question was absurd. A jumbled mess of thoughts invaded Rayna's mind. Did Nazalon threaten their land or had the witch Nadiuska somehow survived and followed Rayna there? She wanted answers but she wasn't ready for the one she received.

"Your battle with the witch awakened the Source Gods," Talakai told her. "There was no volcanic activity as the scholars believed. The God of Fire rose up from way down below and he will not stop until all of Kartha is turned to ash."

Rayna fell back against the bench in disbelief. She stuttered out the first response that came to her.

"The Source Gods...they're not real."

Talakai squatted down and stared at her good eye. "They're very real and they've come to reclaim the world they built from us mortals. But you're special." He tapped the dragoneye resting in the hilt of her sword. "You're the only one who can stop them now. This is your mess to clean up. I'm insisting that you do it. Otherwise, we're all going to die."

~

Beneath the bowels of Kartha, he waited. Deep in the core of the land is where he drew strength. Soon the time would come, and he would decimate all the people of the valley if they did not praise him.

But as he sat in solitude a peculiar energy crossed over the land. A presence he'd not felt in a very long time stepped foot on Kartha and she brought with her a magnificent beast. Perhaps he wouldn't wait so long this time before going up top. He wanted to see Rayna for himself. If the blonde bitch dare show her face where it wasn't wanted he would burn it off.

9

Rise

Rayna recognized her own limitations even if Talakai could not. If the God of Fire truly threatened to burn Kartha to ash their best course of action was to flee the island. Instead, they set her up in a lavish suite trying to convince her to help.

Lilac flowers floated across a milky white bath. An open window let in the cool breeze off the courtyard where meat was being roasted for dinner. A stack of fresh clothes sat on the edge of the bed and next to them her gold and black armor.

Rayna ran her fingers over the grooves of the designs to make certain she didn't dream the experience. When she saw her hand shaking out of fear it told a thousand tales. This wasn't a dream; it was a nightmare. How could she be expected to kill a Source God?

To buy herself time she told Talakai she would think

about it. He didn't seem pleased with her answer but it's the best she could give at the time. They brought her to the private chambers after that. It was a step up from being dragged around before, but they still locked the door.

Talakai didn't lie. He wasn't about to let her leave Kartha until she helped them. If she wanted to, she could climb out the window at dark to escape. But after the fight with the witch, and the fever, she didn't know if her grip would hold. She could fall and break her leg from that height. Then she wouldn't be any service to them and they would no doubt throw her into the sea.

If they meant to sacrifice her to the God of Fire they didn't let on. The people of Kartha worshipped their Source Gods, but ritualistic killings weren't usually a part of the ceremony. No, in Talakai's mind he truly believed Rayna was some sort of god in her own right. How wrong he was.

If he knew half of the things she'd been through since leaving Kartha, he'd change his mind about her being their champion. So why not tell him? Her flaws and losses would convince Talakai she was a mere mortal. Then they could devise a proper plan of getting the people safely off the island. Rayna knew it would be a hard sell to convince them to leave their homeland, but it was the only way they would survive. Relying on her to win the war for them was a fool's bet.

Rayna sat in the bath until the water ran cold trying to come up with a way to convince Talakai to change his mind. She also tried hard to remember her original teachings of Karithik. If she spoke their native tongue the people may be more inclined to listen to her point of view.

The clothing they provided for her wasn't what she preferred to wear. But as a guest she would honor their customs. For the people of Kartha, it was easiest to use the hides of animals they hunted to fashion clothes. It was also a way for them to honor the animal and ensure no part of it went to waste.

Rayna wore leggings made of deerskin leather. A simple, long piece of cloth wrapped around her waist covered her breasts. She fashioned her blonde hair back with a shell clip letting a few of the curls fall across her forehead.

Looking more like a lady and less like a warrior, Rayna went on a mission of diplomacy. As foreign as she was to the land her methods felt even more out of place. Her usual course of action would be to crack skulls and sort them out later. But if they were truly dealing with a Source God, she wouldn't get close enough to strike.

Part of her still denied their existence. She had enough time soaking in the bath to ponder it all. If the Source Gods did exist, why had they waited until now to rise? The entire time the witches, and others, sought the magical beings of the land to drain them of their power the Source Gods did nothing.

Now Talakai expected Rayna to believe that her battle with Nadiuska caused such a ruckus that it woke the sleeping giants. The idea of it sounded like the ramblings of a mad man. That is what she feared more than a made up god.

Madness touched Toth when they were together. Perhaps it ran in the family. Rayna already dealt with a mad king on Atharia. His fevered dreams led her down a path of destruction she could never return from. All that chaos brought her here. If she did believe in the gods, she would ask them if this were a test. Did she land on Kartha to make amends for past deeds or to save another troubled king?

Freshly cleansed and dressed it took Rayna a few more moments to summon the courage to have an audience with Talakai. He seemed steadfast in his resolve that she would be their savior. It was an honor bestowed on her before by many and one she never wanted.

In her best use of the Karithik language she called out to the Royal Watchers on the other side of the door. At first, she received no response, so she tried again. If they left her to rot inside her room then she would have no choice but to escape from the window. She would use the whip of bone to climb down.

As Talakai promised it had been returned to her as well.

The hideous machination came from the dreaded pirate D'zdario Dizdar. Rayna would never commission such a terrible display. But the whip had come in handy for her and it would do the same now.

A sheath was made for Bhrytbyrn. Custom leather with etchings and jewels that represented only the finest warriors on Kartha. It was all too much. They shouldn't be revering the woman responsible for their prince's death. And if Talakai were right, it was because of Rayna that King Krato fell too.

The weight of such responsibility felt heavy on her neck and shoulders. All the healing of the hot bath to soothe her muscles faded as they tensed up again. She rolled her head to relieve the tension then went to the window.

Outside the people of the city continued as if nothing threatened their safety, not even the stranger watching them from above. Some of the children spotted her and waved then continued playing. It was a tight-knit community, but it looked to Rayna as if they'd all grown soft.

Her days on Kartha in the past saw a strong military presence and structure to that force. Now they seemed splintered and aimless in their direction. If nothing else, Rayna could help Talakai bring order to his kingdom.

Toth always wanted her as his queen. Together they were going to rule Kartha with a fair but firm hand.

Then Toth began to change. He lusted for power that did not exist. In time, seeking such things drove him mad and it wound up costing his life.

The memory of that day sat on her heart like a fresh wound. She lurched against the open window and began to weep. Her most exposed moment is when the door finally came open. She stood up straight and wiped the tears from her cheek. Then turned to greet the guards.

It was the same man and woman from before as if they'd become her own personal escorts. The man looked her over with concern then muttered something to the female. She also looked uncomfortable. Perhaps they didn't want to draw babysitting duties for the foreigner.

"No weapons," the girl said.

Rayna looked herself over and realized she wore the whip at her side and sword at her back. She nodded agreement and sat them both by the edge of the bed. The male guard waved her out and she went willingly. As she passed the female guard the girl smiled at her.

"You look pretty."

Rayna felt her cheeks flush. In her best Karithik she replied "thank you" which earned her another smile from the girl. Using their language was already paying off. It made the Royal Watchers feel more at ease in her presence, at least the female. The male guard still seemed uncertain as to why Rayna got such special treatment.

He reminded her alot of Falkon Fourspire, the prince turned King of Atharia.

Falkon hated Rayna from their first meeting. Only in his death did he finally see she wasn't his true enemy. She hoped the people of Kartha discovered that before anyone else died.

She met Talakai again. He waited for her at the bottom of the stairs. As she approached, his mouth fell agape. Shooing away the guards, Talakai stepped up and took Rayna's hand to lead her down the last few steps.

"Thank you." She gave him her softest greeting.

"My pleasure," he replied, kissing her hand before releasing it. "You look absolutely stunning."

"To be honest I feel out of sorts without my weapons and armor."

"We can remedy that."

This time they explored something more to Rayna's tastes. He brought her to the weapons room where they housed their military arms and training area. Rayna marveled at the vast array of unique armaments. The Royal Watchers and the rest of the soldiers guarding Kartha trained with blunt, wooden sticks. They were thick and solid with heavy knots resting at the end of long handles.

Talakai invited her to try one. She was surprised to find no hindrance in the weight of the short staff. It moved with fluid grace in her hand and promised vicious strikes from the gnarled knot on top.

"That's called a batu. They're hand carved from the finest wood." Talakai told her. He could tell she was enamored with the weapon. "I'll have a ceremonial batu made for you...if you do as I ask and face the God of Fire."

Rayna was prepared to give Talakai a strong debate on the approach to their current god problem. She didn't like telling kings how to rule their lands. But when they acted like fools, she had no problem setting them on the right path. Had revenge for her family not blinded her when King Favian came calling, she wouldn't be in this mess now.

In the short span of time after prince Falkon fetched her from a tavern in Theopilous her entire life became upended. Cooler heads and different choices could've remedied that. Rayna made mistakes but she always learned from them. She wanted to tell all of this to Talakai but he caught her off guard with an assessment of his own.

"I've never known you to back down from any challenge, especially when it involves your friends. I think when that witch took your eye, she stripped your confidence as well."

"I still killed her," Rayna argued.

"Yet, you keep balking whenever I broach the subject of the God of Fire. I'm genuinely surprised."

Rayna's grip tightened on the batu. She wanted to strike Talakai across the face with it for his insult until she realized he spoke the truth. Setting the weapon down she sat on a wooden bench set up so warriors could comfortably wait while their boots were mended.

Talakai didn't join her this time. He liked standing over others. That's why the dining area was set up with the patrons inside a small pit while the king's table lorded over them.

Height, weight, strength, none of that usually affected Rayna. She fought dragons most of her young life. How could a mortal man be of any consequence? But this wasn't a man threatening the island of Kartha. It was magic, Source Magic, and that scared Rayna to her core.

"I would help you if I could, you know that," Rayna began. "But you imbue me with skills I do not have."

Now Talakai crouched before her. He opted to fall back on their friendship to convince her. The little boy who followed her and Toth around never did so for his brother. He wanted to be in the presence of the warrior woman as though she were a deity herself.

"You have all of that and more," he said. "Why can't you see it?"

"I only have one eye."

The quick quip made Talakai fall over laughing. When he realized the joke was at Rayna's expense, he straightened up and apologized. She waved him off and tried again to make him understand she wasn't the champion he needed.

"If I fight the God of Fire and fail, he will burn this island to ash anyway. Why not just leave here? Save your people from certain doom."

He took her arm and led her from the armory. Rayna hated to leave so soon. She had only explored a small part of the stock. An entire back wall of native weaponry called out to her. As they passed the array of batus, Rayna snatched one from the table and slid it inside her dress.

"I can't ask my people to leave the only home they'd ever known," Talakai explained. "Where would we go, Ischon? Atharia? No, this is our land."

"I understand it would be difficult..."

"No, you don't understand!" It was the first time Talakai raised his voice to her. "Running away is not the answer. It wasn't the first time you ran from here and it's not the answer now."

Rayna knew it was only a matter of time before he brought up her past on Kartha. The clear blue sky was shifting to gray clouds as a storm rolled in. It seemed appropriate given how the conversation soured. Rayna didn't want to talk about it, but Toth wasn't going to give her the option.

"When Toth died I waited for you to come talk to me, but you just left me here to wallow in my grief." He explained it as though the hurt were fresh in his heart.

Usually, Rayna didn't let guilt control her thoughts. It was a waste of time indulging in such emotions. Things that happened in the past were meant to stay there. But her time with Ryu and her other companions, Jagger and K'lani, back on Atharia made her a different woman.

She wanted to explain to Talakai what happened back then. But if she started talking about Toth the emotion would come flooding back to her. And that is something she preferred not to endure.

"Can you take me back to my room now?" she asked. "My wounds are still healing, and I grow weary."

"Of course."

Talakai indulged her for now, but it was only a matter of time before he wanted her answer about fighting the God of Fire. She couldn't give it, at least not the choice he expected to hear. Laying on her bed and staring at the ceiling she considered her options.

Was Ryu still out there waiting for her or had he given up and left Kartha on his own? The thought of being separated from him again after just reuniting stung. She imagined that's how Talakai must've felt so many years back.

Hurting him isn't something she set out to do back then. Just like she didn't mean to cause him pain now. It was in everyone's best interest that she left Kartha then. Parting now made more sense than facing down a god.

Daring to make moves without guards on her trail, she escaped from her suite. No prison could hold her if she truly wanted out. The only time her jailor kept her imprisoned was when Nadiuska ripped out her eye. At that time, dark magic was involved. Rayna didn't like tangling with magic of any kind. It was too unpredictable.

This time when she slipped from her room, she had no intention of trying to leave. Instead, she made her way to Talakai's chambers. It stood at the top of the stairs behind a large wooden door. The Royal Watchers patrolled the floors below but the hallway directly in front of the king's chamber remained clear.

Rayna used all her strength to climb up the balustrade. Wearing nothing but a loose sleeping gown helped her navigate the climb with ease. She moved with the same subtleties used when tracking a dragon. No sudden movements, just smooth, direct steps. It helped her avoid detection from the guards. She didn't need them interfering with what she was about to do inside the king's chamber.

10

Still of the Night

alakai rested in a large, ornate bed. It didn't suit him. He, and his brother before, enjoyed simple pleasures. The expanse of the cushion engulfed Talakai making him look like the little boy Rayna remembered long ago. She stood over him for a moment watching him sleep. It seemed a restless slumber rather than a peaceful one. He mumbled and fidgeted speaking in Kirithik to an unknown entity. Heavy is the head who wears the crown.

Rayna didn't want to take her next action, but it was necessary to move things forwards. Crawling onto the bed with the slow grace of a cat she straddled him. As he started to wake Rayna reacted swiftly by pinning his arms with her muscular legs. She cupped her hand over his mouth and motioned for silence.

Terror filled Talakai's eyes as he came fully awake. The

trembling of his body beneath her own caught Rayna by surprise. Looking at the situation from Talakai's point-of-view she realized her mistake.

"I'm not here to kill you," she assured him. "I just want to talk without constant interruptions."

He mumbled and tried to nod. The fear hadn't left his eyes, so Rayna kept her hand on his mouth. She didn't need him crying out for the guards until she said what was on her mind.

"It troubles me that you think I abandoned you in your grief," Rayna started. "I did not want to leave you, Talakai. After what happened to Toth your father thought it best that I leave Kartha and never return. The Royal Watchers escorted me to the boats. I didn't have a chance to say goodbye and I'm sorry for that. And I'm sorry for being your champion."

Talakai's dark eyes had softened. It seemed he wanted to say something in response to Rayna's confession. Slowly, she lifted her hand from his mouth. She released his arms and began to slip from the bed when he caught her. Drawing her back Rayna's first instinct was to fight. But when Talakai pressed his lips to hers she unclenched her fists.

His kiss was deep, full of passion and longing built up over the years. He rolled Rayna to her back and kissed the nape of her neck. She tried to reconcile all the reasons their bedding would be a mistake, but desire took over any good judgement.

Only now did she realize Talakai slept naked as his arousal grew more intense. Stripping Rayna of her sleeping gown he paused to stare at her body. She wondered if he noted all the new scars that came from years of battle. Talakai did not seem to mind about that, nor did her disfigured eye bring him pause. He looked at her with awe and softly uttered the word "beautiful."

Then he took her with a roughness that unfortunately made Rayna think of his brother. She tried to push out the memories as he moved inside her only to have them replaced with thoughts of her husband Jagger. Though not a traditional ceremony they still committed themselves to each other. Rayna even had the tattoo across her arm to prove it. Somewhere back on Atharia he awaited her return.

Soon she couldn't focus on anything other than the pressure building inside of her and the intensity of its release. Talakai moaned as he felt her body quiver beneath him. Still wary of the guards, Rayna cupped his mouth with her hand stifling his own climax.

After reaching the peak of pleasure Talakai remained atop her for a moment. Shaking her hand from his mouth he leaned in and kissed her lips. She returned his affections, letting her tongue meet his with slow, sensual flicks.

Talakai shifted to his side but kept his gaze upon her.

He ran his fingers through her sweat-soaked hair and smiled. With her physical pleasure subsiding Rayna grew uncomfortable. This was a man in love. She'd seen it before many times. The feelings were not requited, and she didn't want to upset him.

Instead of speaking, she smiled back then turned over as though she were going to sleep. Talakai moved closer and wrapped his arms around her. He held her so close to his body she could feel the rhythm of his heartbeat.

Bedding Talakai was a big mistake. He was lovesick; he always had been. Now that they'd shared their bodies Talakai would seek her hand as his queen. That isn't something Rayna wanted. There was only one thing left to do now. When Talakai finally fell back to sleep Rayna slipped from the castle and headed back to find Ryu.

11

What Lies Beneath

er movements angered him. The warrior woman left the castle of sticks in haste. Rayna intended to flee rather than fight. This could not be. She meant to take the magnificent beast back across the sea. He would not allow it. A stretching of his arms shook the very foundation of the island. After 800 years the God of Fire awakened.

~

Fully clad in her armor, with her weapons in tow, Rayna raced down to the beach. The dark of night made it difficult to discern whether she traveled in the right direction or not.

It felt like weeks, not days, had passed since she and Ryu set down on Atharia. Wounded and weary, she did not have a strong sense of direction then. Only instincts carried her. They managed to lead her astray, right into the path of the Spirit Watchers.

Now her head was clearer, the wound at her side healing, and her body thoroughly relaxed. Her instincts were stronger now and they would guide her back to Ryu.

Rayna liked to think she held a strong bond with the dragon. In the past, the dragoneye curse from the witch helped her find dragons to slay. Now, even with the eye gone from her head, she still felt that inexorable tug that told her which path to take.

She started up a mound of sand, certain it would lead her to the hilltop and hopefully Ryu. As she dug in her heels the ground itself started to shake. At first, Rayna assumed it was the trembling of horses upon the ground. The Spirit Watchers had spotted her and were heading out to bring her back.

But the way the sand shifted around her feet told her otherwise. It felt as though the beach had become a quicksand pit. She started to sink down as the sand swallowed her. Rayna felt a pulling from the very depths of the island trying to drag her through the earth.

Struggling to free her whip of bones she used it to lash against a nearby piece of driftwood. The muscles in her arms bulged as she strained against the invisible force below. Her hands chafed trying to stay locked upon the handle of the whip. Then it slipped from her grasp.

She cried out as her body sank to the waist. Clawing at the sand in panic Rayna didn't know what to do as she continued sinking lower. She screamed hoping the Spirit Watchers were close by. Better to deal with them than whatever force had hold of her now.

The guards didn't come to her aid, a familiar friend did. Swooping down from the night sky Ryu called out to her. Overjoyed to see her dragon, and more than awed at the size of him, Rayna reached up the best she could.

Ryu lowered down just enough that she could grab hold of his tail. As he began to fly the ground shook again causing Rayna to lose her grip. She fell back down into the sand almost to the neck. Ryu's calls of frustration echoed across the sky as he circled back around.

Rayna could see he intended to land. She waved him off in fear for his safety. Using all the strength she could in her finely honed body she pressed up from the sand. Torso free once again she reached out and got hold of her whip. Ryu noted her intentions and continued flying.

On his next pass over her, Rayna snapped out the whip. It lashed around Ryu's hind quarters good and tight. Once he felt the whip in place, he spread his wings wide and shot up towards the sky. Rayna hated heights. But being buried alive was even worse.

She dangled off the back of her dragon as he flew skyward. Clutching the whip for dear life, Rayna kept her eyes shut and trusted that Ryu knew where to bring them for safety. A moment later Rayna tumbled to the ground as Ryu set them down upon the hill where they initially began the journey on Kartha.

Rayna fell upon stacks of animal bones picked clean of meat. Ryu had become hungry and fed on a wide variety of stock. She scanned the bones to see if any human remains were visible and grew relieved to find none.

Scrambling to her feet she rushed to Ryu intent on hugging his massive neck. He bared his teeth and screamed with such force it blew back her hair. She turned towards the source of his discontent only to find the entire army of Watchers, both Royal and Spirit, surrounding them.

Talakai headed them up on horseback. Both he and his steed were heavily armored. No hide armor suited their king. His was fashioned of studded leather and scales not unlike Rayna's own. The boy watched and learned all her tricks back then only to use them against her now.

"You think I'm foolish enough to fall for your feminine wiles?"

"What're you talking about?" Rayna shouted, putting herself in front of Ryu as Talakai approached.

"I knew you didn't bed me because you cared for me," he said under his breath, so the others did not hear. "You did it so you could sneak out."

His accusation, though partly true, burned her ears.

She wanted the chance to explain but the aggression on all sides was too high.

"It wasn't my intention," Rayna told him. "You initiated it."

"Of course I did," Talakai admitted. "I wanted you to lead me here to your dragon."

He snapped his fingers and the lot of soldiers surrounding them began throwing chains upon Ryu. He fought them off but grew overwhelmed by the numbers. They even dragged him down as he tried to fly off.

"It didn't have to come to this, Rayna," Talakai told her. "But if you don't face the God of Fire, I'm going to take your dragon."

Any semblance of guilt or regret Rayna held for past deeds left her with Talakai's threat. Seeing Ryu struggle under the weight of chains made her enraged with the need to protect him. Instead of going after the guards who held him down, she sought their leader.

Taking the stolen batu from her belt she launched it into Talakai's forehead with such force it took him off his horse. Before he even landed Rayna was upon him. This time while she straddled him, she rested the blade of her sword across his throat.

"Make no mistake, Talakai, if harm comes to my dragon, I will kill you."

With her sword on the soft flesh of their king the guards didn't dare advance. They stood with weapons drawn waiting for the opportunity to strike Rayna down. Should that time come, she intended to take as many with her as she could.

Their king, laying helpless beneath the pale-faced intruder, suddenly grew somber. He lost all his bravado and began to weep. Rayna recognized his tears were not from fear. No man on Kartha feared death. This ache he showed ran much deeper.

"Please, Rayna," he begged. "You're our only hope to defeat the God of Fire."

"Why do you keep saying that?"

"Because it's Toth. The God of Fire is my brother Toth."

12
The God of Fire

She backed off him wondering if island madness took over his mind but knowing in her gut that it hadn't. The moment she let her guard down the Watchers attacked. Several men and women from the Royals grabbed Rayna and dragged her off their king. The Spirit Watchers continued holding Ryu as he struggled to help his caretaker.

Talakai sprung to his feet shouting at them to stop. They either didn't hear him or directly disobeyed his order. Rayna felt clubbing fists atop her head, into her ribs, and across her wounded side. The daring and outrageousness of attacking their king brought out a vicious side to the Royals Watchers.

Rayna covered her head trying to absorb the blows with her arms. Each time she reached for her sword a strike made it through her defenses. Before Talakai managed to pull them off her a solid punch caught her across the jaw. It bloodied her lip and made her blackout for a brief second.

In the darkness of unconsciousness, she saw Toth there. He smiled at her, extended his hand, then burst into flame. Regaining her wits, she lashed out at Toth only to realize it was just a vision. A memory of the past or a warning of the future she did not know.

Talakai knelt in front of her and tried to assess her wounds. She pushed his hand and backed away. Searching for Ryu she stumbled to her feet only to fall into the waiting arms of the Royal Watchers.

"Take her to the medicine huts," Talakai commanded.

"No!" Rayna argued and struggled as the guards took her arms.

"Gently," Talakai told them. "She's to be treated with kindness not malice."

"I'm not going anywhere until you release my dragon."

Talakai's eyes flitted to the side where Ryu remained held down. He grimaced at the sight of the dragon then turned back to Rayna and shook his head.

"What's to stop him from burning all of us alive should I let him go?"

"You have my word...for the dragon and the God of Fire."

"Does that mean you'll agree to help us?"

Rayna spat a mouthful of blood that inadvertently landed on Talakai's boot. He looked down in disgust then back to Rayna with concern. She let him wait a moment longer before giving him the answer he had sought since the first.

"I will help you kill your brother."

~

He could've taken them all then. Scooped them up in a ball of fire and batted them around like a child's play toy. Better to wait and see his puppets dance on their strings. Except for Rayna. None could tie her down. Toth tried years before, but she rejected his ideas as the ramblings of a madman. Now she would see how wrong she was to say such things.

~

The medicine women Aga and Linae tended to Rayna's cuts. She understood their Karithik scolding when they told her to stay out of trouble. The older one, Linae, even used fruit to show her concern.

"Next time, squish!"

Using a ripe melon, she smashed it in her palm. Rayna nodded her understanding. The women treated many injuries in their day. Rayna carried the scars of several lifetimes. Linae worried if she continued fighting in such a manner that her head would eventually be beaten to a pulp.

Throughout her travels Rayna saw soldiers with such

head wounds. They could no longer speak correctly. Some couldn't even feed themselves. Should that day ever come she would gladly finish her life on her own accord. The women should've set the melon on fire. That seemed a more appropriate fate given she agreed to face an unbeatable god.

When Talakai came to check on her later she only had one thing to say: "Where is my dragon?"

"He's unharmed. We've given him food and water." He paused and rung his hands as though suddenly nervous in her presence. "Thank you for ordering him to stand down."

"You don't order a dragon, Talakai," Rayna explained. "You ask him nicely and then if he wants to listen to you, he will. Otherwise, he'll burn your damn village to the ground."

"The dragon will, or you will?"

"Toth is the one you should be concerned about. How could you not tell me about him sooner?"

"I was trying to find the words to explain."

"You thought fucking me would loosen your tongue?"

Her remark brought giggles from the medicine women. To this, Talakai ordered them to exit. He closed the door leaving the two of them alone in the hut. Rayna gently touched her bruised face then mocked him.

"I'm a little sore to be going around again. Perhaps if the King of Kartha bent the knee to me first."

She crossed and uncrossed her legs to emphasize her meaning. Talakai glanced at her sex then grew frustrated with the vulgarity of the act.

"Shut up, Rayna!"

"Why? I'm going on a suicide mission to try and free your people from eternal fire. I should be offered whatever I wish."

Mindful of her aching body she moved with ease from the bed. Slapping it with her palm she continued to push Talakai with her inferences.

"Or do you want to just bend me over right here?"

He stepped towards her, invading her personal space. For a moment she thought he might be foolish enough to try and force himself on her. Instead, he retaliated with words that stung worse than a slap in the face.

"I love you, Rayna. I always have. If you felt as though I treated, you as a whore in my chamber I am terribly sorry." He bowed his head. "I've wanted you for a very long time. But it's no excuse."

She lifted his chin and glanced a kiss off his cheek. "You take all the fun out of taunting you. I enjoyed myself as well. Do not think otherwise. But you still should've told me about Toth. This changes everything."

"I thought if you knew the true identity of the God of Fire you would not want to face him."

Rayna took his hands in her own. "I need to face him. But first, you must tell me how Toth could've become a

Source God."

Talakai gave a heavy sigh as though fearing this very moment. He motioned towards the bed for her approval. With a nod they both sat and Talakai began to tell her of Toth.

"You remember back in those days when you were at Toth's side how he would chase the rush?"

"Yes, it's one of many reasons he didn't want the throne."

"Then what happened?"

"You know as well as I do."

"No, Rayna, what do you remember from the day Toth died?"

She didn't want to recall the memory. It was something she'd locked away in her mind never intending to seek it out. Now, as Talakai insisted it was important to the events at hand, Rayna went back there to that fateful day.

"The rush of conquering physical feats no longer appealed to him," she began, her voice shaky. "Toth told me he wanted to breach the realm of magic. To pierce the dark veil that no other could and in doing so become a vessel of source magic."

Talakai encouraged her. "Go on."

She grimaced and turned her gaze from him. Her eye filled with tears as the last moments with Toth came rushing back. Voice breaking, she recalled the events leading up to his death.

"He studied every tome he could find. Spoke to the medicine women and mages. Toth even discussed his ideas with strangers to your shores. In all his research he got it into his head that he could do as he said: break the barrier between the world and the sources of magic."

Sensing her distress, Talakai took her hand and squeezed it. Body racked with sobs Rayna held onto him as the emotions of the past caught up with her. She felt like a tiny ship awash in a storm at sea.

"I begged him to stop," she said through tears. "Magic is not a thing to be trifled with. But he wouldn't listen to me, Talakai. He made trades with seafarers to collect as many books on magic as he could. Then he kept trying to cast spells that would grant him access to the other side. Until one day it consumed him. His mind went first. Obsessed with reaching his goal I didn't even recognize him anymore. He grew thin and short-tempered. But in his madness, he believed he found the answers.

I watched helplessly as he cast spells he muddled together. Soon they started to take effect on him. I tried to intervene, but he threw me to the ground, and I feared he may kill me. The dark magic had overtaken him but not in the manner Toth wanted. Desperately, helplessly, I watch it burn him up. At first, Toth seemed overjoyed as though he wanted it to happen. Then, I heard him screaming in such a way that it still echoes in my ears. Toth burned away to ash that day."

She let the rest of the words fall out of her like plucking an arrow from the breast. The initial pain seethed as though it would be unending but once the shaft was removed from the flesh it started to heal. At the conclusion of her story, Rayna looked up at Talakai. He fought back his own tears trying to be strong for her.

Talakai patted her hand and wiped her tears. He stood and smoothed his tunic as he began to tell Rayna his side of the story. In the aftermath of the events King Krato had banished Rayna from the island. He blamed her for the death of his first-born son saying that her wild spirit infected his boy with a lust for power. Once Rayna left, she never wanted to think of Kartha again.

"But Toth did not die that day," Talakai began. "In my grief I foolishly wanted to follow my big brother to the grave. I began doing research on exactly what happened. What I found out scared me straight. But I continued to look into the details in secret. My father would hear none of it. In his mind he'd dreamed up a scenario where you killed Toth. I never believed that."

The warmth of his smile comforted Rayna even though the tale he told was building to the unimaginable. After her experiences with magic on Atharia she knew great power existed. Even her companion K'lani spoke in favor of the God of Wind. But if the gods did exist, she needed to learn how Toth took the mantle of God of Fire. That is what Talakai explained now.

"Somewhere out of reach from the living, and beyond the veil of death exists a darkness. Many amateur witches and mages have tried to pierce the veil in the past. Those that succeeded were driven mad by the depths of this darkness. You see them in taverns to this day rambling to themselves; their minds broken from things unfathomable to the human mind.

But there are others with certain energies that can conjure powerful spells. However, if they're uneducated in the way of casting, the spell will overpower them. The magic takes control and eventually changes the spellcaster into something different."

"What do you mean it changes them?" Rayna asked. "I saw Toth burn alive."

Talakai shook his head. "No."

"Yes," Rayna argued. "I had both eyes at the time, Talakai. I know what I saw."

"Toth was one of the rare users of magic who broke through the veil," Talakai went on. "That day when he wouldn't stop conjuring the spell consumed him. Too much magic ran through him until it was the only thing left. His mortal body was burned away as you saw but he wasn't dead...only lost."

Suddenly an unexpected spark of hope churned in Rayna's heart. She hopped from the table and began pacing with fevered energy. Thoughts raced through her mind as she pieced together what Talakai was saying.

"If he's lost then we can bring him back!" she exclaimed.

Talakai didn't share her excitement. "Rayna, once Toth became this being of pure magic he sought and destroyed the original God of Fire. That is how he secured the mantle as a Source God. He killed the original and took his place. Trying to restore him to human form isn't the answer. My brother is dead. What's left in his place is an unstable, wild magical force."

"Have you even tried, or did you just assume it wasn't possible?"

"Of course, I tried to save him. Toth is my older brother. But what's happened to him is unknown and unstudied. Only a handful of published works have even the slightest amount of information on spellcasting gone wrong. What I've learned myself is that Toth is no longer inhibited by mortal rules. He runs off impulse alone. That makes him dangerous."

"Toth was always impulsive," Rayna recalled. "You wanted me to help you with your god problem. I believe it's possible to restore Toth back into a human."

"Rayna you're going to get yourself killed," Talakai said as he took her hands in his own. "That's not why I asked for your help. I truly believe you can defeat Toth in battle. You have the skill."

"If you love me, and you love your brother, you'll let

me try to bring him back rather than kill him."

The guilt Rayna felt over Toth's death stayed with her for years. Now the chance to change all that lay at her feet. She only needed to have the courage to try it. Stranger things had happened in her life. Who would've thought to see a dragonslayer befriend a dragon? Rayna reconsidered when it came to Ryu. She could make Toth turn as well.

"You need a source of power strong enough to face my brother," Talakai said.

"Good thing that I do," Rayna smiled. "Now take me to my dragon."

~

His was an increased capability of all that magic entailed. In the days after becoming the God of Fire, he began to understand the functions and hierarchies of the world as they related to the rules of magic.

As a Source God, he was able to perceive magic to a deeper and more profound degree than any witch or magician. He could perform more complex magic without the need for intricate, time-consuming rituals.

The distinction of his power was vast. A complicated spell which took a skilled magician years to learn was solved in the snap of a finger. He could travel on wisps of air or his preferred choice of fire.

They wanted to take all of this away from him.

Returning to human form would leave him stuck and unable to enjoy the world as he did now. They thought him to be bloodthirsty, that all Source Gods were attributed this type of behavior.

Toth didn't feel the urge to kill anyone, but rather, wanted to be free to do whatever he wanted and perform beautiful magic. They would not take that from him.

~

Ryu was healthy but agitated. He didn't like having the guards so close to him. Talakai kept a group of them to keep watch as though they would be able to stop the young dragon should he act up. But Ryu remained calm as Rayna had instructed. She rewarded her good boy with a rub on the nose and a fresh leg of lamb.

Talakai remained close by as well. He was in awe of Ryu but also a frightened. Rayna motioned him forward. At first, he hesitated but at her insistence he came closer. She took his hand and gently set it on Ryu's neck. Rayna felt Talakai trembling and tried to reassure him.

"He won't attack you if I don't command it," she said. "We have an understanding."

"When you were here before you spoke of eliminating all the dragons of the world."

As Talakai told her tale she felt Ryu's energy shift. The dragon glared at her in a manner which she'd never seen before. Rayna knew it was only a matter of time before he found out her true past as a dragonslayer. Now was not that time.

"I was mistaken," Rayna said, more to Ryu than Talakai. "A misguided pledge made by a sorceress that controlled me like a puppet."

"I'm glad you cut your strings," Talakai said in jest. "But is a dragon going to be enough to face a Source God?"

At this remark, Ryu chuffed air from his nostrils that blew back Talakai's hair. It startled the King of Kartha and made him leap out of harm's way. Rayna couldn't help but laugh at the sight.

"Ryu's insulted by your lack of faith."

"Tell him I didn't mean it!"

"Relax, Talakai," Rayna insisted. "So much time on the throne has taken away your sense of humor."

"It's not so amusing when your brother wants to burn you alive."

She took his hand. "I won't let that happen."

"You may not have a choice."

Rayna looked back at Ryu. He blinked at her with his large eyes as though already understanding what they needed to do.

"I should face Toth alone," she said.

Talakai grabbed her shoulders and squared her to him. "No, Rayna. I'll have my army at your back."

She shook her head. "I can reason with Toth. He'll

listen to me."

"Don't you understand? He isn't Toth anymore."

"If that's the case then it will give you enough time to get these people off the island."

Before he could argue further Rayna kissed him. Talakai wrapped his arms around her and held on tight as though he never wanted to let go. The man truly did love her. Rayna's calling was not as a queen but a warrior. She knew what must be done to quell the God of Fire.

13
The Power You Seek

Talakai gathered seasoned warriors and the most knowledgeable tacticians to his court. None of them knew how to summon the God of Fire. Perhaps they didn't try too hard to find him. Or maybe Toth didn't want to be located. Rayna knew where he would be.

Going against the travel order, and ignoring Talakai's pleas for her not to, Rayna went to the forbidden part of the island. There on the shores she and Toth used to spend most of their days together. They would swim, hunt, and explore both the island and each other. Headed there on Ryu's back, Rayna remembered those times with fondness. She only hoped Toth shared that sentiment.

Sitting upon Ryu's back as he carried her across the sky didn't get any easier for Rayna. Talakai commissioned a saddle be made to rest on the dragon's back. Ryu didn't like it at first, but he allowed Rayna to place it upon him so it would ease her journey. It didn't.

She hoped in time she would get used to the dizzying feeling. For now, she gritted her teeth and steadied her breath as he glided over the trees. With each turn he made, Rayna gripped the horn of the saddle so tightly her hands began to perspire.

As the ocean came into view, she considered abandoning the quest and heading home to Atharia. It was a fleeting thought. She couldn't break her promise to Talakai and she needed to face Toth. Even with so many years gone Rayna would never forget the bond they once held.

She motioned Ryu towards the city by the sea as it came into view. This is where the original castle stood. The people of Kartha held more prominence than they did now. The city used to be bustling with activity but as Ryu flew closer Rayna saw nothing except the wreckage that remained.

Just like the fallen Laihaka Valley that burned to the ground, the city had fallen. Even the stone structures that once stood as guard towers were in disarray. Every bit of the city had been charred or demolished like a child throwing a fit and breaking his toys.

Not a child, a man. Yet not a man. An entity of pure magical energy. He waited there for her in the center of the city as though he knew she would come. Rayna hesitated to have Ryu get any closer. She instructed him to settle down on the outskirts of the city where the gates used to stand.

Once she slipped off the saddle, he made a mewling sound as though he begged her not to go. She rubbed his thick neck and tried to assure him that she'd return soon. They both knew it was a lie.

Rayna kept Bhrytbyrn sheathed. The bone whip and batu each hung from her belt. She didn't want to approach in an aggressive manner. That would only cause Toth to react in defense. Rayna hoped to speak with him the way they used to. She opened to Toth in a way she never could with anyone else.

As she approached him now her breath caught in her chest. Toth retained his physical appearance as she'd known him years before. Except now he was even more beautiful. Magical energy coursed through him replacing the blood in his veins. It made his skin glow brightly with a blueish tinge.

Daring to step closer, Rayna felt the immense heat emanating from Toth's body. Wisps of smoke trailed up from his skin and occasional bursts of white-hot flame licked his cheeks. Sweat dampened her brow and her back though the island air was crisp. Toth watched her approach. His eyes and mouth lit up distinctively with magic flames then dissipated into billows of black smoke.

"Toth, it's so good to see you after all this time," she said with a smile.

"You're talking as though you mean something to me."

His voice sounded the same as Rayna remembered though distant as if echoing from inside a well. He looked at her with his strange, dark eyes but didn't recognize her.

"My name is Rayna," she explained. "It's been a long while, but we used to be very close once."

He waved her off. "I know who you are, silly girl. You just don't mean anything to me."

His words stung and stopped her forward movement. She didn't need Toth to care for her as he once did but if he held no regard for her at all then talking him down would be useless. Rayna looked back towards the gates where Ryu waited for her. She wondered if she could outrun a Source God. Fleeing the scene of a fight wasn't in her nature. But if something went sour during these talks she needed to regroup. Still clinging to hope that her tactics would work, Rayna tried again.

"I didn't mean for any of this to happen to you, Toth."

"What happened to me?"

Was he toying with her, or did he truly not remember? Rayna tried to broach the subject as delicately as she could. With trepidation in her steps, she moved closer.

"You were overtaken by a magic spell," she began. "Your body couldn't hold that much magic. It burst into flames and consumed you. I watched you die."

Suddenly he was nose-to-nose with her. She felt the bursts of flame coming from his body lick her skin. The heat poured off him and into Rayna rivaling any dragon's breath.

"Did I die, or did something more happen that day?"

Toth reached out a finger to stroke Rayna's chin and she pulled away. Her reaction caused him to laugh with a childlike glee. Then he appeared behind her whispering his hot breath upon her ear until it sizzled.

"Interestingly, I didn't feel the flames at first. It confused me but then as my mortal coil began to burn away, I felt serenity. Everything I'd been chasing to that point made sense. The only thing that mattered was accepting my transformation into the being you see before you now. I couldn't move as my physical body converted into pure magic, but I saw everything. Even as the bright flame enveloped me in its power, I saw you, Rayna. I watched you run away in fear."

"I went to get help," she explained.

"You ran away and left me there alone."

He spoke in such a way it sounded as though it pained him to remember. Against her better judgement Rayna reached out to Toth only to have him singe her arm and then laugh about it. She drew back in pain and instinctively set her hand on the hilt of her sword. Toth watched her clutch Bhrytbyrn and it soured his mischievous mood.

"You've always been a marvel in this mortal world, Rayna. But my power far surpasses your limited human experience. Such opposition is pointless. Don't fight me, join me as I wanted you to do so long ago." He let a glowing orb of fire hover over his palm. "Let my fire envelope you and burn your essence into paradise."

Rayna was shocked. "You want me to die?"

"How many times do I have to tell you I didn't die...I transcended."

Only now did it become clear what Talakai tried to warn her about. This wasn't Toth. In his lust for true power, he'd burned away his body and spirit to become a darker, more disturbed version of himself. Killing the original God of Fire and taking his place further enhanced his transformation. Rayna no longer saw anything that resembled the man she once loved.

"What are you?" she asked in disgust.

The being that was once Toth shook his head as though he pitied Rayna. He started juggling his fireball from hand-to-hand as an expression of his power. She wasn't impressed, nor did she fear any longer. Rayna was only trying to keep Toth occupied while she came up with a new plan.

"What I've become clearly is beyond your comprehension," he said. "I exist in a realm that far exceeds your pointless physical world. Mine is an endless source of energy that can build or destroy as I see fit."

"If you feel such contempt for our world why bother with it?"

"Because that's a part of my nature now. As the God of Fire, I belong to a race far older than your kind could ever understand. You acknowledge us with ceremony and scripture, but you don't truly know us. Even those days of worship are exceedingly rare. Once the four of us Source Gods ruled this world. It amused us to watch the antics of you pathetic wretches. But I grow bored of sitting at the side. Now I want to revel in watching you squirm."

Rayna couldn't believe what she was hearing. "But these are your people, Toth."

"They were my people. Now, like you, they mean nothing to me."

"Even Talakai?"

At the mention of his brother's name, it appeared as though Rayna were finally getting through to Toth. The flames licking up from his skin snuffed out. His glowing eyes flashed back to the dark hazel coloring she remembered so long ago.

Rayna took another step, arms outstretched trying to welcome Toth into an embrace. Her hope lay in the bond of brothers. If she convinced Toth to reconcile with Talakai it would be a start. However, if she couldn't he would burn her the moment she touched him.

"Surely you don't want harm to befall your brother," she continued.

To this, Toth laughed. "Oh, but I do. The same way I harmed my father. And the same way I'm going to harm you!"

His eyes lit up again in gold flame. Fire burst up from his body like a freshly lit torch. Rayna stumbled back shielding her eyes from the flames. As Toth became more aggressive she went for her sword, Bhrytbyrn.

Not only a massive blade, but the weapon could also ignite with its own fire. Rayna would gaze upon the sword with her dragoneye to cause the flames to release from it. Now, with the dragoneye embedded in the hilt, she simply traced the jewel with her fingers to call for the fire to appear.

Her enemies fled in fear when the flames came to her blade. But Toth stood back and laughed in amusement. He wagged his finger at her in what she assumed would be her last warning.

"Fire to fight the God of Fire?" He quipped. "You haven't learned much in your travels, have you?"

He was right. Bhrytbyrn wouldn't help her now. Ryu came from behind her blasting Toth with a stream of dragon's fire. It only seemed to charge the fire god even more. When Ryu made his appearance known that is when Toth finally attacked.

He let a stream of fire flow from his fingertips summoning it from the depths of his being. It circled through the air in a direct line towards Rayna. With no other protection she held Bhrytbyrn up hoping it would deflect the flames. Ryu had other ideas. He extended his large leathery wing out, catching the fire just as it reached her.

The dragon squealed as he felt the impact of the attack. Hearing him in pain angered Rayna and she reacted like a mother protecting her young. With Toth focusing his attention on Ryu it gave Rayna the opportunity to stage her own attack.

Ducking under Ryu's wing, and the blast of fire being doled out by Toth, Rayna made her move. She swung down on the God of Fire with everything she held in her body. He stopped her before she could connect. Catching her by the throat he taunted her.

"You cannot hurt me with your puny weapons."

Rayna felt the skin of her neck burn as Toth lifted her higher. She defeated dragons, a witch, and countless creatures of the night. But Rayna didn't know how to defeat the God of Fire. As he laughed at her dismay, she thought back to all her training trying to seek the answer.

It wasn't in her training where she found what she needed. The lore itself told a thousand tales. On Atharia, all magic came from a source be it fire, water, earth, or air spells. Magic began to wane when the source no longer presented itself on the land. If Toth was the source of fire magic, Rayna needed to snuff him out. No source magic meant no more God of Fire.

She would start with basic elemental knowledge. Taking the water satchel from her belt she sprayed it into Toth's face. As the fire extinguished it left a blast of steam behind that scalded Rayna's arms. She winced from the pain but continued to hold the water on Toth until the entire satchel drained.

He dropped her to the ground and tended to his face. Black plumes of smoke billowed up from his head as he shrieked in pain and panic. Rayna took a minute to assess her own damage. A few more scars would cover her body, but nothing would keep her from finishing what she started.

The water would only work as a distraction. She knew Toth would regenerate his powers in mere moments. Rayna couldn't let that happen. She needed to act swiftly before the God of Fire was back to full power. Scrambling to her feet she took a chance and leapt onto Toth's back.

The flames of the God of Fire were diminished, and Rayna intended to keep them that way. Wrapping her arm around his throat she squeezed with all the strength she could. Ignoring the pain from her tender, burned flesh she would suffocate Toth and snuff out his flame for good.

He struggled to breathe but still held enough strength to loosen her grip on him. That gave Toth enough wiggle room to call forth what looked like fire bats. They circled Rayna trying to burn her arms so she would release their master.

Keeping one arm around Toth's neck she took the whip of bones from her belt. Each time she lashed it at the bats they disintegrated into ash. But with each bat eradicated another took its place. Then Ryu came to help her.

The dragon took the attention off Rayna as the bats attacked him instead. He let them get just close enough and then flew up into the air causing the bats to chase him. With the distraction eliminated, Rayna used the whip on Toth instead.

She wrapped it tight across his throat and even covered his mouth. He struggled trying to spark up more flames but when fire lost oxygen it could no longer live. Rayna squeezed until his body turned gray and collapsed. She rolled away from him and grabbed her sword once more. Standing over the smoldering pile of remains, she waited for him to rise again. But the God of Fire was no more.

Rayna felt her heart ache and tears streak her face. In her mind she saw the encounter going another way. She hoped reuniting with Toth would bring her back in time to the moments when they were genuinely happy together. Instead, it came to battle and another fallen comrade. Then his body moved.

She readied herself for another fight. If he started to get to his feet Rayna would have to make a move that would haunt her for eternity. But even gods couldn't exist without a head. Sword held high she got ready to decapitate her former lover.

"I'm so cold," he muttered, struggling to get to his knees. "You drained all my fire. Why would you do that to me?"

"Because you're a menace just like any magical being I've ever come across," she told him. "You needed to be stopped."

Toth fell to his back too weak to stand let alone fight. He stared up at her with eyes cold and dark. Rayna saw no fire god yet no sense of humanity either. He was a withered husk. A body without a soul. Still, he tried to taunt her.

"If that's the way you feel about the Source Gods, you're in for a surprise."

"Are you trying to scare me?"

"No, I'm trying to warn you," he said. "The rest of the Source Gods won't be so easily defeated. I'm still new to my powers and position but Persea, Cebrios, and Thealia have been around for centuries. You won't be able to stop them from rising and taking over."

Deep in her gut Rayna knew the other Source Gods were coming. And if her battles with the witch Nadiuska prompted their return she felt a responsibility to try and stop them. But Toth spoke the truth. The other gods held immeasurable powers. A twinge of hope filled her heart as she broached an impossible suggestion.

"I could stop them if I had help."

His dark, lifeless eyes stared at her as he gave an emotionless response. "We once meant something to each other. I remember that now. But without my powers I'm no help to you."

"Are you asking me to charge you up with flame?"

Toth gave a weak smile. "I'm tempted. But I couldn't say for certain that I wouldn't turn around and try to kill you again."

Rayna bowed her head. "I'm so sorry it came to this, Toth."

He reached his hand to her. Certain he no longer posed a threat she sheathed her sword and knelt beside him. Clasping his hand in her own Rayna wanted to pull him close to her. But the moment they touched Toth's body crumbled to dust.

Rayna cried out in anguish as she tried in vain to hold him together. Soon she found herself pouring through nothing but ash and sand. The remnants of Toth drifted up on the air and through the fallen town. Rayna imagined his spirit was finally going to rest alongside his father.

She stood and watched the last wisps of ash float away. The wind circled them around as though Toth were dancing. With a tear in her eye Rayna saluted her lost love.

"Be at peace, Toth."

14
Unburied Past

A banquet was thrown in her honor. She and Ryu dined like royalty for stopping the threat to Kartha. Then, as she expected, Talakai asked her to stay and be his queen. Rayna turned him down. When he asked why she told him about the other Source Gods.

"I can help you." He gripped her hands as though he could hold her there.

"No, Talakai. I need to go back to Atharia and find my companions, Jagger and K'lani. They will help me. This isn't your fight."

"But I love you," he told her. "Whatever battle you're facing I will stand by your side."

Rayna kissed him then shook her head. "The people of Kartha need you here. Rebuild the city by the sea, honor your father and brother. In time, you'll forget all about me."

"Not likely."

He held her in a comforting embrace. Rayna never liked getting too comfortable. As the night's festivities wound down, they went to bed together. One last evening of pleasure before Rayna sought her next adventure.

Talakai was gracious enough to give Rayna supplies to return home to Atharia. She strapped what she could to Ryu's back using saddle bags. He huffed in discomfort, but they came to an agreement. Then it was Rayna's turn to get on his back. She slowed her breath and tried not to think about the impending flight across the sea.

"They make herbal remedies for that," Talakai joked.

Rayna blew him a kiss then waved to the onlookers. The medicine women Aga and Linae held a special place in her heart for their care. Perhaps someday Rayna would return to the island to see them all again. For now, she and her dragon left Kartha. Ryu took flight slowly at first then he increased his speed and they set off for home.

~

The travel back to Atharia started smoothly. Rayna conversed with Ryu throughout the flight. Even though he couldn't yet speak, she picked up nuances from his sounds that made sense to her. It was nice to have a moment just between the two of them. They'd been on the run for so long it didn't give them much time to bond. But they forged a special relationship anyway.

"Forged in fire, aye Ryu?"

As Rayna called to him there was an unexpected answer. The dragon didn't speak. A voice from the depths of the seas sounded out instead. Suddenly Ryu balked and reared back almost sending Rayna spilling off into the ocean. At first what halted him looked like a giant tower of waves. Then the water began to take the form of a person, or more accurately a goddess. As Toth warned her, Persea, The Goddess of the Sea had come for Rayna.

"So, you can kill Source Gods." Her voice boomed across the expanse of the sky.

Hovering there on Ryu staring out at the vision of water made woman, Rayna was in a precarious position. One swat from the goddess and it would send both down to the ocean floor. She lifted her voice and shouted so the goddess could hear her.

"The God of Fire gave me little choice," Rayna explained. "But I have no quarrel with the rest of the Source Gods. So long as you crawl back into your holes."

To this Persea laughed. "A mere mortal giving an ultimatum to the creators? That amuses me."

"Your lot seems very easily amused. Or touched in the head, I can't tell which."

"I'd say you are the one with impending madness if you expect to face me and live."

Rayna held her ground. "As you said, I've killed a god before. How difficult can a water witch be?"

"Water witch?" The goddess took this as an insult. "Witches stole their powers from us! We are not the same."

"I've defeated a witch as well," Rayna told her. "She didn't care for your rules. In fact, she's the one that woke you...not me or anyone else on these lands."

Ryu was starting to wane. Rayna needed to wrap this up whether through bypassing the Goddess of the Sea or by blood. She readied Bhrytbyrn in her hands. If water took out the God of Fire, then it would make sense that fire be the Persea's weakness.

"This is true, you did defeat the witch Nadiuska for us."

Rayna corrected her. "I did it for me."

"Either way you did us a favor. She was growing troublesome. But I still can't let you pass."

The Goddess of the Sea insisted on a fight. So be it. Rayna stabled herself on Ryu's back to take her sword in both hands. She rubbed her palm across the jeweled hilt and woke the flames resting inside.

As Bhrytbyrn sparked up she pointed it towards the Goddess of the Sea in challenge. Persea flicked her finger out causing a splash of water to cascade over the two of them. Ryu had to struggle to remain steady as the water bared down on his wings. The wave quickly extinguished any flames from sprouting off Rayna's blade. She was surprised. The fire inside Bhrytbyrn came from powerful magic. It wasn't something that could be doused easily.

"Your flames cannot harm me. I'm of source magic," Persea explained, then she sent out a warning. "I could drown you both just by taking you in my hands. So, don't try that again."

Rayna pushed back her wet hair, regained her position on Ryu, and ignored Persea's warning. She extended her sword tip towards the goddess in challenge. Persea took the act of defiance with grace and rather than drown them, she accepted. Rayna readied herself to face another god, but the terms of the battle were unexpected.

"I like you Rayna," Persea said. "I do not wish to kill you but as I said, I cannot let you pass either."

"Seems we're at a standstill then."

"No, there will be a battle but in the effort of fairness I shall use a proxy."

"You fear me Goddess of the Sea?"

As the words escaped her lips Rayna knew she shouldn't have said them. Persea splashed them again for Rayna's insolence. This time the water drove the pair tumbling down through the sky straight towards the ocean. In the sprawling sea they'd be no match for

Persea.

Rayna shut her eyes and braced for the slap of the water on her skin. Instead, she felt the grain of wood break her fall. They remained at sea but somehow managed to land on a boat. As Rayna stood and looked around, she realized it wasn't just any boat she accidentally boarded. This was The Widowmaker, a famed pirate ship helmed by the infamous D'zdario Dizdar.

The last time Rayna saw Dizdar they'd used his lifeless body to punch a hole in The Widowmaker to escape. Now he stood before her again. His skin appeared muddied with patches of it missing. Multiple wounds riddled his torso where her companion K'lani had stabbed him. The once silken, dark hair now looked gray and brittle. But his eyes told a thousand tales.

No longer did any life shine behind his pupils. Only milky white orbs stared back at Rayna. But they did indeed stare. Dizdar was transfixed on the whip of bones at Rayna's belt.

"Mine," he moaned through a withered mouth.

Escaping from the Widowmaker, she gathered whatever weapons could be found. Dizdar's slaver whip was among them. It came in handy for Rayna many times since then. She wasn't about to give it back.

"You want it? Come get it."

Dizdar wailed a piercing cry that hurt the ears. But he

didn't yet advance. Behind him more dead pirates began to shuffle out of hiding. Soon the entire crew of the Widowmaker stood there facing down Rayna and Ryu. No matter, Ryu could burn them all back into their crypts with one breath. But the Goddess of the Sea had rules to this fight.

"No crew, no dragon," she said watching from above them. "Just you against the pirate captain."

Rayna looked the long way up to face her. "How do I know you won't interfere yourself?"

"You have my word," Persea told her.

The word of a Source God meant little to Rayna. She never found them useful in the past. Now that they'd come to reclaim their world they were even more of a problem. Rayna would deal with Persea afterwards. For now, D'zdario Dizdar was her focus.

In life, the man was strong and swift. Rayna hoped his waterlogged death took those skills from him. But the walking corpse was being controlled by the goddess herself. Persea could imbue him with whatever special traits she wanted. Rayna would have to prepare herself for anything.

Out there floating in the middle of the ocean upon the dilapidated Widowmaker, the fight began. Rayna waited for Dizdar to make the first attack. He moved with staggered steps at first giving Rayna hope that he'd lost his human skills. But when he drew close enough,

Dizdar became shockingly fast.

He blindsided her with a strike to the temple causing the patch to fall from her ruined eye. Dizdar looked her over and laughed. His voice churned as though water filled his throat as he spoke.

"You look even more hideous than I remember."

"Have you caught sight of yourself lately?" Rayna quipped. "You're not quite so dashing anymore, Dizdar."

He frowned and touched his shriveled fingers to his face. His thumb caught a loose piece of skin that peeled off and fell onto the ship's floor. Dizdar fumed ripping more pieces of skin from his face.

"What happened to me?"

"You're dead," Rayna advised. "Look around, this is a ghost ship now."

Dizdar glanced at his crew who stood lifeless at the helm. Then his torn face turned back to Rayna. His jaw and cheekbones protruded through the ruined flesh. The milky eyes looked her over no doubt taking in her healthy flesh tones and the breath lifting her chest.

"If I'm dead you're coming with me."

He rushed towards her. Rayna hoped to use his haphazard advance in her favor, but Dizdar was much quicker than anticipated. He caught her in the belly with his shoulder and lifted her up. Feet dangling beneath her, Rayna struggled against the capture. Dizdar would not be stopped. He rammed her back first into the side of the ship. The impact knocked the wind out of her. As Rayna struggled to regain her breath, Dizdar took back his whip of bones.

He lashed the whip of bones across Rayna's torso. The strike of the blow reminded her of day one on his ship. She'd been sold as a slave to Dizdar, and he made certain she knew it by whipping her with the human spine. Rayna's body still held the scars.

When he lurched back for another strike, she dove at him. One lash with the whip was enough to know she never wanted to feel the spiny protrusions on her skin again. She and Dizdar struggled with each trying to get the upper hand. Rayna knew he'd been strong in his human life, but this seemed otherworldly. Persea was guiding her puppet.

Rather than continue a losing battle of strength, Rayna devised a new plan. She let Dizdar have his whip and went for her sword instead. He wouldn't let her go so easily. Tossing the whip out again it caught Rayna by the ankle causing her to land chin first on the deck.

She heard Dizdar's chuckling grow louder as he approached. Shaking the pain from her jaw, Rayna readied herself for an attack. The moment she felt his hands at her feet she kicked him in the mouth. He staggered back but only for a moment; then he was on her again.

As he bent down to clutch her throat Rayna used the batu to crack Dizdar across the face. The wooden knot at the top shattered Dizdar's already ruined face. His jaw split in half and his cheek sunk inwards as the bones splintered.

Watching him clutch at his wounds Rayna was relieved to discover the dead still felt pain...at least in this instance. With the opportunity open she got hold of her sword and lit it up in fire. Bhrytbyrn glowed in a magnificent hue of amethyst flames from the blade.

Rayna twirled the massive sword in a circular motion overhead. The fire whipped around as though it were a living entity. When she built up enough energy Rayna slashed out with Bhrytbyrn. A ball of fire ejected itself from the blade in her attack. But she didn't aim it at D'zdario Dizdar; instead, Rayna set her sights on Persea.

The fireball cascaded up as though launched by a catapult. Distracted by her champion's ruined jaw, the Goddess of the Sea didn't notice the fire coming her way. It struck her in the chest and instantly her body evaporated. A hollow scream echoed through the sky as the Goddess of the Sea was conquered. In the wake of her death Dizdar and the other pirates began to burst like pierced water bags. Rayna saw the destruction and hurried over to Ryu.

"We have to get off this boat!"

Hopping onto Ryu's back the two of them lifted just

as The Widowmaker began to dissolve into nothingness. As Ryu pressed on towards Atharia, Rayna looked back over her shoulder to ensure Persea did not remain. No water witch pursued them. They were safe until the next Source God showed up.

15

Home Sweet Home

Anytime Rayna's travels took her abroad she always returned to Theopilous. Seated at the tavern with feet stacked on the table, a mug of ale in hand, and a pipe between her teeth is when Rayna truly felt at home. Off instinct, she directed Ryu towards what some referred to as the "town of thieves." Given how many scoundrels frequented Theopilous the name suited it well. Rayna didn't mind the company. It let her fit in undetected and she could gather her strength in peace.

As they came off the water and into Atharia the air felt different, sweeter somehow. Rayna took a deep breath and allowed herself a moment of peace before the chaos found her again. Ryu seemed to be enjoying himself as well. He dipped and swirled through the sky rather than flying frenzied with worry about attack. Rayna started to grow accustomed to the motion of it. So much time on

Ryu's back was breaking her fear of heights. But even with their shared moment of joy she knew there would be those eager to fight her dragon.

King Favian's bounty had been lifted from her head, but Rayna would still face challengers. It had been that way since she earned the moniker of dragonslayer. Tough guys looking to test themselves, and mercenaries wanting to fetch a fee, would try to fight her. She didn't want Ryu to endure that same situation. Rather than parade him through town she would have him stay hidden inside the Fickle Forest.

The area got its name from fables. People claimed to see creatures lurking within. Once the stories grew it kept travelers from heading through the forest out of fear. Truth be told no monsters lived within those woods. The only thing to fear were thieves taking all you owned. Her husband Jagger and his men the Forsaken Force made a career out of it. But even they no longer claimed the forest as their own.

Now the Fickle Forest belonged to Ryu. The fables had come full circle. There really was a creature lurking there. A dragon that almost stood tree height and which could kill without mercy or remorse. Unless Rayna deemed it as such. For now, the only order she left him with was to be safe and defend himself when needed. Other than that, she let him be a young dragon and hunt the forest for food.

While Ryu ate and rested Rayna needed to do the same. She walked the deserted path from the Fickle Forest to the town of Theopilous taking the time to appreciate her homeland. As she neared the entrance to town, she fashioned a new eyepatch. The lot who lived and worked there wouldn't even notice her missing eye. Everyone in Theopilous had their own sad stories. But Rayna would rather not have to explain herself should the question arise. All she wanted was a cold beverage and a night's rest.

Stepping through the doors of the tavern she realized that her wishes would have to wait. Inside smelled the same with fresh baked bread in the air. Lively music came from the local lute player while dancing girls entertained each table. Everything was the same as Rayna remembered it. Even the patrons inside were recognizable.

One man at the bar stood out above all the others. He wore his hair shorter than she remembered. The line of his strong jaw hid beneath a bushy beard. But the hue of his blue eyes was unmatched.

A part of her wanted to run to him. Another part warned her to approach with caution though she didn't know why. She called Jagger's name over the noise. When he turned to face her, Rayna discovered why she felt concerned.

His brow furrowed and his eyes went cold. At first, she

feared Jagger was overcome by one of the remaining Source Gods the same way Toth had been. But his anger came from a more dangerous place: a broken heart. He drank back the rest of his beverage and then stomped towards her.

"You left me."

"Jagger, we don't have time for this."

"I thought you were dead."

"I need to find K'lani, where is she?"

He blinked in agitation. "You returned for her? Are you two lovers? Were you fucking her behind my back?"

On each question Jagger's voice grew louder. Even with the bustle of activity in the tavern, his shouting caught the attention of onlookers. Rayna didn't want to cause a scene, nor did she need the townspeople knowing her business. But his line of questions stirred something in her that caused an immediate response.

Tired, frustrated, and insulted by Jagger's accusations she slapped him. Her sudden attack prompted a quick response as Jagger struck her back. This caught the attention of a nearby group of warriors. A rough and tumble man with a shaved head inserted himself in the altercation by shoving Jagger back.

"We don't take kindly to men assaulting women here." The bald man looked Rayna over and raised his eyebrows in admiration. "A woman with her build is clearly formidable, but that still doesn't give you the right to strike her."

Jagger didn't hesitate to retaliate. Using a clay bowl from the bar top he smashed it over the bald man's head. The blow cut his flesh and dropped him to one knee. Standing over the stranger, Jagger continued his shouting.

"Stay out of it!"

His assertive demand didn't go unchallenged. The man who Jagger assaulted wasn't at the tavern alone. His four companions stood from the table so fast it almost tipped over. Like most patrons of the tavern, they'd all been drinking heavily; that included Jagger. Once the first blow landed a massive altercation ensued.

Jagger held his own against the quartet even though they outnumbered and outweighed him. He threw over chairs putting obstacles in their path so they couldn't reach him. In their scramble to avenge the bald man a few of them bumped into another group and spilled their drinks. This caused more men to join the fray. Soon an all-out brawl erupted.

Rayna sat back and watched from the bar as bodies were hurled over tables, drunken punches thrown, and chairs smashed. The tavern owner, Talos, yelled for them to stop. He even stood on the bar top and shouted at the fighters.

"They can't hear you," Rayna told him. "Best to let it play out."

"They're going to destroy my bar, my livelihood." His eyes welled with tears as he pleaded with Rayna for help. "Please, Rayna. Do something!"

Talos always took good care of her when she came through town. Seeing him in despair made Rayna's heart ache. She couldn't just stand by and watch the tavern get torn down. Where would she go to drink if that happened? So, she joined the fray.

Rather than throwing blows she threw bodies, starting with Jagger. Grabbing him by the belt and tuft of hair, Rayna tossed him out the door. By now the massive bald man who came to her aide was back on his feet. He followed Jagger outside intent on exacting a measure of revenge for his bleeding head.

As he straddled Jagger and readied his fist to strike, Rayna intervened. Even though they were quarreling she wasn't about to let her husband's pretty face get smashed in. With a swift kick to his back, she knocked the bald man over. Seeing this, his companions once again came to his side as two of them tackled Rayna around the waist.

All of them went spilling to the ground outside in a massive pile. Their exit from the tavern caused the rest of the brawlers to either follow them out or settle down. It wasn't exactly how Rayna wanted to save the tavern, but it would do. Now she needed to save herself.

The two big men pinned her to the ground. One held

her face against the hot sand while the other moved to defile her. This brought Jagger running to her aide. He dove atop the man and started banging his head against the ground. The other, surprised by Jagger's vicious attack, took his attention off Rayna. A mistake. She pulled his hand from her face and bit his fingers until the smallest digit tore off in her mouth.

Wailing in pain, blood spraying up from his damaged hand, the man fell to his ass. The tall bald man ran to his side wrapping his hand with a cloth to staunch the blood. He saw his other friend laying in a bloody mess as well while both Rayna and Jagger stood victorious over them. The man grimaced and directed his anger at Rayna.

"We were trying to help you"

"I didn't ask," she replied.

He spat at her prompting Jagger to try and continue the fight. Rayna caught him under the arm and pulled him back. The fighting had subsided all around. There was no sense continuing the brawl when more important matters needed attention. Rayna tossed a few coins towards the men trying to make amends.

"Ale is on me."

Even though their gallantry was misplaced she wanted to thank the men for their effort. She also knew that Talos' tavern could use the extra coin. At first, they hesitated to accept the gift, but men of their ilk didn't often pass up a free drink even if it meant swallowing their pride. They gathered the coins and headed back inside the tavern. Jagger tried to follow as though her invitation included him.

"No," she said, catching his arm again. "You've done enough damage."

"You're placing the blame on my shoulders? Typical."

"What does that mean?"

He shrugged her hand off. "It means you don't take any responsibility for your own actions. You never have."

Rayna couldn't tell if his anger revolved around her disappearance from Atharia or if it were wrapped up in their past. Either way she needed it to be settled. Back on Kartha she refused Talakai's help because she believed her companions would join her fight. Now it seemed Jagger would rather fight her instead of their common enemies. She wanted to explain the gravity of the situation with the Source Gods rising. But he started to walk away without hearing her words.

"I need your help," she said.

"Keep it," he called. "Whatever tale you're going to spin I don't want to be involved. I'm through risking my life for you."

"You made a commitment to me, Jagger," Rayna reminded him displaying the ceremonial ink on her forearm. "We made a commitment to each other. Are you going to walk away from that as well?"

Their shouting caught the attention of onlookers. Some snickered at the display while others called for them to "shut up" or "take it inside." Rayna ignored them all. Her focus remained on Jagger. He turned around and came back to face her. His words came out wrapped in raw emotion she'd never seen him exude before.

"Don't you dare talk to me about commitment. I watched you fly away on that damn dragon while you left me to die. Now you come back here acting as if nothing happened. You left me first. So, yes. I'm choosing to walk away now."

"And that's typical of your behavior," she told him. "Back when your father died you found it easier to blame me. You cast aside anything we meant to each other rather than dealing with your pain. It seems nothing has changed."

Jagger waved her off and kept walking. Weaving back and forth with shoulders slumped, his gait told a thousand tales. Intoxicated, beaten, and sad he tried to keep his head up. Jagger remained a proud, stubborn fighter no matter the situation. Rayna wanted to call to him but couldn't find the words to make him understand without inciting a riot. Before he staggered out of sight, she took a deep breath and set everyone around on high alert.

"There's a war coming."

In a town like Theopilous it took quite a bit to grab the

attention of those that resided within. Talk of war turned a few heads but no one truly reacted with much concern. Even Jagger brushed her off with a quip.

"What else is new?"

He laughed then found his way to the brothel house. Pausing at the door he looked back to make sure Rayna saw him enter. As if carousing with whores made a difference to her. But when he disappeared inside Rayna was surprised to find it did matter. She grimaced at his drunken display but chose to focus on preparations for the other Source Gods. Now that the Goddess of the Sea showed up Rayna knew the others would be coming.

So far, she bested two of the gods. But part of her knew she was as lucky as she was skilled in their defeats. When the God of Wind and Goddess of Earth came calling, she wasn't sure if luck would hold. Having backup on her side of the fight would be more than helpful. She needed the ability to brainstorm with those she'd already been through war with. Now that Jagger turned his back on her, Rayna lamented rejecting Talakai's help.

Still, she had Ryu. If one needed to go into battle against a god, then a dragon made a fine ally. She could also try to reach out for K'lani's help. To do that she'd need to locate the girl first. Was she even still on Atharia? That was a quest Rayna wasn't quite ready to take on. Now that the altercations and anger simmered, she returned to the tavern for the drink she wanted for initially.

Talos welcomed her in and thanked her for stopping the fight. He tried to offer a free beverage for her efforts. Rayna insisted on paying until she realized all her coin went to the big men now seated in the back with their drinks. She thought about apologizing again for biting off the brawler's finger. Instead, she took her free drink and slunk to the back of the room to her usual table.

The man was lucky she didn't rip off a different appendage with what they were trying to do. Rayna shook her head in dismay. Everywhere she traveled someone either wanted to fight her or fuck her. Sometimes they wanted both.

As one of the bar maidens passed by, Rayna sought a pipe and tobacco. The woman provided what she could: a misshapen clay pipe and a few flakes of herbs.

She smiled and left Rayna to indulge in her smoke. Taking her time, she loaded the clay pipe with the flakes, set it to her lips, then passed a candle beneath the bottom of it. After a few puffs she began to enjoy the taste. More importantly, Rayna was able to relax.

Leaning back in her chair, feet stacked on the table, she let ringlets of smoke rise from her mouth. The last few days started to catch up with her. Fighting a witch, crashing on Kartha, battling two Source Gods and then her own husband. All of it took a toll on her body and mind.

She felt a deep ache in the muscles of her shoulders and lower back. The wound at her side healed over but remained tender to the touch. Rayna knew she couldn't continue her journey without a good night's rest. With Ryu safely tucked away in Fickle Forest she could lay her head down without worry for just a little while. When she woke the final two Source Gods would be her focus.

16

Unity

Talos gave Rayna the same room she always accepted when arriving at Theopilous. It was small and modestly decorated with only the essentials like a bed and a bath. She lit up a torch then set her weapons out across the bed. Standing over them she marveled at the collection she was beginning to gather during her travels.

Bhrytbyrn was her first. A fine blade gifted by her father to Rayna when she was still very young. That massive broadsword saved her life on more than one occasion. The whip of bones sat twirled around itself giving the spine an "S" shape.

When she first cast her eyes on the gruesome device of torture it made her ill to think how many perished to fashion such a whip. But the way it moved with such sleekness began to charm her. Besides, her broadsword held an amethyst jewel that once sat inside her own eye socket. A whip made of a human spine matched well.

The batu was a fine replacement for the dragon dagger she once carried at the small of her back. That dagger was claimed by her traveling partner K'lani in an act of thievery. Rayna didn't mind. Call it a gift just as the batu was a gift taken from Kartha that she would always remember fondly.

Alongside the weapons sat her armor. The set included a full breastplate, greaves, and gauntlets all polished in black and gold. They were forged by a master craftsman and taken from the palace of Saltwood Stronghold. The armor previously belonged to a man she knew only briefly but who'd become a good friend. Valerios died trying to help Rayna.

He left behind a fiancé, K'lani's sister Kemi, on the island of Ischon across the sea. She owed Valerios a debt of gratitude strong enough to travel to Ischon and tell his bride the truth of what happened to him. Besides, given everything she knew about the girl, that is where K'lani would've returned to.

It would be a long, arduous trip across the sea and one Rayna had never made before. She needed rest and to gather fresh supplies in the morning. There was no telling what awaited her on that venture. It made good sense to be extra prepared. For now, she snuffed out the torch flame and lay atop the bed with Bhrytbyrn only an arm's reach away.

During the night, a rustling at her door caused her to sit up. She took hold of her sword in both hands and softly eased herself from the bed. Some fool was at the door trying to pry it open. Of all the rooms along the corridor they picked the one with a warrior cranky from lack of sleep.

She did not want a fuss or a long fight. Instead of waiting for the thief to pick her lock, Rayna opted to let him in. She would give him a fright and sound thrashing then move him on his way. Holding Bhrytbyrn aloft she swung open the door which dragged in her would-be thief with it. He staggered on drunken legs and fell at her feet.

Rayna looked at his soft blue eyes staring up at her and lowered her sword. It was Jagger, stinking drunk and absently wandering into the wrong room. She picked him up and dragged him to the washing basin where he pooled cold water across his face.

"This isn't your room, Jagger," Rayna explained as she stood by the open door waving him out.

"I know it isn't. I don't have a room here."

"So, you thought you'd just bunk with me?"

"Why not? You're my wife."

Jagger crawled atop her bed and tried to settle himself there. Rayna slammed the door startling him awake. She stomped over and tried to drag him from the bed. He shook her hands from his legs and scooted further back.

"You're not staying with me," Rayna told him. "Go back and sleep with one of your whores."

He shook his head. "I'd rather sleep with you."

"That's not happening."

Jagger slid from the bed and came towards her. Rayna pushed him back, but he remained undaunted. Reaching out again, he delicately brushed her cheek with his hand.

"I didn't bed any of those women."

"Why not? Couldn't afford them?"

Rayna tried to joke but she sensed a heaviness in the air. It ran through Jagger's fingertips into her skin and permeated her chest. The weight, she realized, was tied to their relationship. It ebbed and flowed over the years like a ship upon a stormy sea. Now, as Jagger tried to steer them back to something calmer, Rayna made a confession that would upend them.

"I slept with someone else."

Jagger dropped his hand from her cheek. "Who?"

"A man on Kartha. A king," she admitted. "It was a mistake."

"You were on Kartha this whole time?"

"Yes, when Ryu flew us out of the Majestic Mountains, he went so far across the seas we ended up on Kartha. I was wounded, Jagger, we both were. If not, I would've steered us home. Once we were on the island many things happened that I don't care to speak of." She lowered her head feeling shame for the first time. "But I thought you should know the truth."

"Because you suddenly wanted to act noble?" He was angered. "I wish I would've fucked those working girls. In fact, there's a couple waiting for me at the brothel right now."

Jagger brushed past her and went for the door. He tore it open and stood there. Rayna didn't turn to see him leave. She simply watched the moonlight pull his shadow across the floor. Then the door slammed shut. An ache in her gut felt like a steel blade was twisting around inside.

She didn't want him to go but she wouldn't stop him either. Then she felt his hands on her shoulders, his breath on her ear. At first, his touch upon her skin made Rayna jump. She thought he may snap and try to strangle her. But Jagger's actions, though fierce, were made of passion rather than anger.

He wrapped his arms around her body as he kissed the nape of her neck. One hand rested on her breasts while the other slid down to her sex. Rayna reached back and gripped his short tuft of hair. Jagger pulled her arm behind her back then bent her across the table.

Rayna let him lead the way. He took her roughly letting out all his aggression through the act of their love making. It roused her in a way she'd not felt with Jagger before and caused a scream to slip her lips. Her audible pleasure spurred Jagger on to his own climax. The force of their coupling caused the table legs to give way and sent them tumbling to the floor.

Sweaty and satisfied the two of them couldn't help but laugh. Jagger dragged himself onto the bed and offered Rayna his hand. She welcomed it and he pulled her close to him. They matched up the ink on their arms signifying their unity. But as they lay there in the dark Rayna couldn't help but feel as though this was the last time she would ever see Jagger again.

17
Scars Run Deep

Waking in Jagger's arms felt comforting until Rayna remembered that the Source Gods still lurked out in the world. They couldn't be bargained with. They wouldn't listen to reason. Only a battle in blood could keep them from taking control of the world once more.

Rayna never much cared for the world. Her desires were driven by a singular purpose: to find and kill every dragon on Atharia and beyond. Now that she no longer walked as the dragonslayer she found there were people and things worth fighting for.

She thought about slipping from the bed and leaving Jagger in peace. But she'd tried that routine before only to have him follow her into a war that wasn't his. Knowing he'd do it again she opted instead to tell him what they were up against. Given all the information perhaps he'd make a smart decision. Rayna needed backup in this fight, but she also didn't want Jagger to get hurt.

Part of her wanted him to step aside. She would never ask him to do that. His pride and protective nature wouldn't allow him to run. They'd both been raised by Darius the Dreaded, leader of the Forsaken Force and a mighty warrior. Darius may have stolen his share of gold but still held integrity in his decisions. Those values rubbed off on his only son, Jagger, and Rayna as well.

She turned over and kissed her husband. It roused him in many ways, and she allowed herself to indulge in their lovemaking again before the battle ahead soured the mood. This time when they came together it was soft strokes and tender touching as their bodies stretched out in long-lasting passion.

Rayna felt warm and safe in Jagger's embrace as though they joined more than just their bodies. She stifled her scream, but her body shuddered from the release. Jagger held her close to him for a long while after they finished. He could sense the impending doom before she even related the tale of the Source Gods. He brushed back the golden curls of hair from her ear and whispered to her: "I love you, wife."

"I love you, husband," Rayna replied, glancing a kiss off his cheek.

Then it was time to leave the imaginary safety of the

bed. Source Gods would wait for no one. Rayna made herself a warm tub trying to decide the best way to approach the subject of impending doom. Jagger slid in next to her with noticeable trouble.

Only now, with the light of day sprinkling down from the window, did Rayna see the scars on his body. Burns puckered the flesh of his arms and torso where the witch Xara struck him with magic flames. The attack left damage that was more than skin deep.

Rayna watched as Jagger's hands inadvertently shook. If she noticed the twitch before her mind must've assumed it came from overindulgence of ale. Now she saw the results of mortals battling dark magic. She reached out and took his hands in her own.

"I'm so sorry."

Jagger kissed her knuckles as they rested atop his. "Don't be. I knew the risks that came with loving you."

He tried to joke but without his swift reflexes Jagger was no longer capable of picking a pocket let alone carrying a sword into battle. His identity was wrapped up in his skills as a warrior and thief. Now Rayna understood why he started drinking so hard.

When her dragoneye was ripped from her head, Jagger had been there to provide comfort and understanding. He brought Rayna back from a darkness that threatened to consume her. She didn't know how to do the same for him now.

Slipping from the tub she dressed and gathered her weapons. To her surprise, Jagger did not follow her lead. Rayna turned around and found him still stretched out in the bath looking up at her.

"You're leaving again, aren't you?"

"Yes," she replied. "

"Then I guess there's nothing left for me to say."

"I have to find K'lani," Rayna explained. "There's a powerful force threatening the end of the world and...."

He cut her off. "Doesn't matter. There's always something."

Rayna sensed his frustration. She gnawed on her lip trying to find the right words to say. Her thoughts and feelings were better expressed through actions. Still, she wanted to try and reach Jagger. She knelt by the side of the bath and stroked his arm. As her fingertips touched his scarred flesh he pulled away.

Rayna frowned. "I won't be gone long."

"Whenever you're done seeking adventure you know where I'll be."

She didn't know whether to feel hurt or relieved that he wasn't trying to stop her from going. In her heart she wanted Jagger with her...always. But her head knew that if he joined her in his damaged condition, it could cost his life. Rayna gathered her things and looked back at him. His deep-set blue eyes seemed to sparkle as he returned her gaze.

"You could come with me."

She knew if she didn't ask, he would resent her for it. Let the decision be Jagger's. He stepped from the bath, water caressing his torso and dripping across the floor as he came to her. With shaky hands he took her face and kissed her forehead.

"I'm no help to you now."

The words slipped through gritted teeth as though it pained him to speak such things. Rayna threw her arms around his neck and held him tight. His wet body soaked into her leathers, but she didn't care.

"There has to be something we can do," she whispered. "A healer or magic."

He pushed her back and took her hands. "Let it be, Rayna."

"I can't when I'm the one responsible for what happened to you."

"What're you talking about?"

"If I hadn't dragged you into my mess...."

"You didn't drag me into anything," he explained. "I'm a grown man and I make my own decisions. I'd do it all over again. But I cannot go with you this time knowing you'll be distracted with worry over me. Better to swallow my pride and stay behind. Besides, that dragon of yours is all the backup you'll ever need."

"I need you too, Jagger...always."

He squeezed her hands. "You better get going."

Jagger glanced a quick kiss off her lips then stepped away to dry off. Rayna fought back tears watching his damaged hands shake as he dressed.

"I am sorry," she told him again.

"Don't be sorry. Just come back."

It took every ounce of energy inside her to leave the room. Once the door closed behind her, Rayna didn't look back. She dried her tears on the back of her hand and then went to gather Ryu.

If she intended on making it to Ischon to find K'lani there could be no more hesitation. K'lani's knowledge of Source Gods would be imperative to have in the battles to come.

18

The Emperor's Daughter

From the hillside K'lani sat beneath a large spring blossom tree and watched the Khai soldiers train. They struck men made of straw with long bamboo staffs. The soldiers all remained in perfect step with each other.

After a while K'lani saw it as more of a dance than a fighting technique. Their footsteps moved with fluid grace. The arc of the staff glided through the air on each swing. But when the bamboo struck the training dolls it created a snap that echoed into the surrounding canyons.

K'lani leaned forward trying to observe every strategic motion they made. She jotted down the steps in a small journal. Alongside detailed drawings, she left herself notes Captain Khadan shouted to the Khai as they trained.

While she drew the next set of steps a large shadow

cast over her. At first, she thought it to be her sister Kemi. But since learning of her fiancé's demise, Kemi rarely left her room. No, the person standing behind K'lani is the one she despised more than any on Ischon.

"It's against the law to reveal the secrets of Khai training."

"I wasn't going to release it to the public, Zhayn," K'lani said not bothering to look up. "It's for my eyes only."

"Wrong, it's only for the Khai."

Zhayn reached down and snatched the journal from her hands. When K'lani tried to get it back he toyed with her by dangling it within reach then yanking it away. It had always been that way between the two of them.

Growing up together they were like brother and sister. Because Zhayn was a few years older he enjoyed teasing K'lani. Even though he'd grown into a tall, muscular fighter he still held the same childish wit. But K'lani couldn't say anything about it. Zhayn was the son of her father's closest ally and a seated member of the council. Even if she did tell her father, he would side with Zhayn.

It didn't matter. K'lani was used to doing things for herself. After meeting Rayna, the famed dragonslayer and aiding her in a quest, K'lani grew more confident. It helped her to hold back tears when her father scolded her for leaving Ischon without permission. She kept her tears back again as Zhayn's taunting grew more frustrating.

"Give me the journal, I need it."

Zhayn tucked the small booklet under his arm. He squared his jaw and narrowed his eyes. K'lani could tell he was being serious then.

"This isn't a joke, K'lani," he told her. "You cannot expose training secrets to the public. What if someone got their hands on this?"

"Please, Zhayn. There are private things in there. Things I've written about my mother."

At the mention of the Empress, Zhayn's eyes softened. He relinquished his obsessive need to follow the rules and handed back the journal. K'lani quickly packed it away before he changed his mind.

"Don't let anyone else see you with it," he said. "And don't come up here again. If Captain Khadan spots you, it won't end well."

K'lani caught Zhayn's arm as he was leaving. He looked down at her fingers grazing his forearm then raised his eyebrows in question. Lower classes were not allowed to touch royalty. Even though Zhayn's family didn't sit on the throne they still held the respect of Emperor Kivu Kazu. Thus, the people of Ischon regarded Zhayn and his family in the highest esteem. Daughter of the emperor or not, K'lani was a class lower than Zhayn. Realizing her mistake, K'lani released her grip and bowed.

"Apologies, Zhayn."

"You don't have to worry about formalities, we've known each other too long for that," he replied. "Besides, you're the emperor's daughter. I should be bowing to you...but I won't."

"That's just it, Zhayn. I want to be more than just 'the emperor's daughter.' Will you talk to Captain Khadan for me?"

"About what?"

"Joining the ranks."

"Not this again!" Zhayn threw his hands up in the air. "I thought you would've learned your place after returning from Atharia."

"The only thing I learned is how cruel my father can be."

"He's trying to keep you safe."

She shook her head. "He's trying to keep me in line."

"Dear, sweet K'lani, there are things happening in the world that you don't understand," Zhayn told her. "Trust that your father is doing what he thinks is best. A little tough love will be good for you."

He could see by the soured look on her face that she didn't agree. K'lani never did like obeying the rules. She acted out a lot in her early years to take the attention from her older sister. As the first-born air to the emperor, Kemi was doted on day and night. Her sister still garnered all the attention though she did little to deserve it. But K'lani no longer acted out for attention. Hers was a hunger to do more for her people and herself. Except no one believed that she could. No one except for Rayna.

Zhayn gave her a light squeeze of the shoulder. "I'll mention your interest to the captain. But I make no promises that he'll listen."

K'lani wasn't expecting his change of heart. Perhaps Zhayn saw something in her as well. Or he just felt sorry for her. Either way, she needed someone on the inside to speak with Captain Khadan. The last time K'lani tried to bring up her interest he ignored her like nothing but a shadow on the ground. Zhayn held rank. His words would be heard.

"I will not hear of this abomination any longer!"

Dinner was meant to be a peaceful time when the royal families would get together and share bread. But Emperor Kivu Kazu's foul mood spoiled any sense of splendor. K'lani couldn't blame her father for all his yelling. She blamed Zhayn for going back on his word and telling her father of her wants rather than asking Captain Khadan to train her.

"No daughter of mine is going to wield a weapon," Kazu went on. "You're meant to find a suitable husband and continue the bloodline."

"That's Kemi's role, father," K'lani argued. "She may be at peace with such a life, but I am not."

The emperor sat back down and sipped his wine. He motioned for K'lani to sit as well. She obliged him but she knew he wasn't finished arguing.

"You've been different since returning from that filth that is Atharia," he told her. "Never have you spoken to me with such insolence."

"I mean no disrespect," she replied. "I'm simply fighting for my chosen path."

"Your path is chosen by me and when you stray from that path you do indeed bring me dishonor."

"Father, perhaps it's better to listen with an open mind to what K'lani is trying to tell you."

"I don't need your help, Kemi," K'lani snapped at her sister.

"Clearly you do," Kemi replied.

Emperor Kazu slammed his fist upon the table causing the plates to rattle. A few cups fell prompting the chamber maids to rush over. Zhayn managed to save his wine from falling. He sat back and sipped it as the arguing continued. K'lani wanted to throw her plate of food at him but felt such a childish act wouldn't help her cause.

Seated around the low table on woven mats were many of the dignitaries who lived on Ischon. Emperor Kazu often invited them as guests to his home to proffer new deals. Her father always preferred dealing in business to family matters. K'lani knew if she continued to argue during dinner the punishment would be severe. Instead, she excused herself from the table and walked out.

Rather than return to her bed chamber, K'lani stormed through the courtyard of the castle. She tugged at the embroidered sash on her waist and removed her fancy tunic. Since traveling with Rayna on Atharia, K'lani came to learn the benefit of wearing more comfortable clothing.

Beneath her royal garb she had on a plain cotton jerkin with matching trousers. Unbeknownst to anyone, especially her father, K'lani brought back armor and riding boots that stayed hidden away in her room. Removing the layers of clothing and loosening the tight braid in her hair let her find relief.

At dinner she felt as though she were suffocating under a life that no longer suited her. She longed to return to Atharia alongside Rayna, Jagger, and little Ryu. But once they separated at the magical town of Mako, K'lani lost track of their whereabouts. She had little choice left but to return home. Now back on Ischon she felt stuck again.

As she stomped through the courtyard, she could hear Kemi calling after her. K'lani didn't want to hear another lecture, especially not from her sister. She tried to ignore Kemi but in her lack of planning she wound up running into a watch tower that blocked her path. By the time she decided which direction to pivot towards, Kemi caught up to her.

"Sister, why do you stomp off like a child when you don't get your way?"

"Why do you keep meddling in my affairs as though you're mother?"

The painful look on Kemi's face made K'lani wish she could swallow her words. They lost their mother, Helena, when they were little. As the older of the two, Kemi remembered more of what she was like. K'lani often pelted her sister with questions about their mother trying to find a sense of who she was as a woman. If Kemi had taken on those traits, it wouldn't be a bad thing. K'lani tried to tell her that as a form of apology but she couldn't get the words out.

"I understand your rage," Kemi told her. "But we can't become as savage as those on the nearby island."

"I'm not a savage."

"You're acting like one. Better still, you're acting like father. Two stubborn bulls unyielding in their stance. Diplomacy is the preferred choice when trying to get your way...remember that."

"Is that how you get everything you want?"

Kemi gave her a forced smile. "If I had everything I wanted then I'd be married right now."

Her words stung K'lani's heart. But her pain didn't measure to the grief Kemi must be feeling for the loss of her fiancé. Telling her sister and her father the details of Valerios' death was more daunting than any battle K'lani ever faced.

Relaying this information is one of the reasons why her punishment had been lenient. But K'lani would've taken a thousand lashings if it meant not hearing her sister wail the way she did. For days afterwards Kemi would sob in her room. Only recently did she emerge but K'lani could sense a difference in her.

"Valerios died a hero, you know that," she said, trying hard to be a comfort to Kemi in that moment.

"This isn't about me, little sister, it's about you settling down."

"I don't want to settle down. Why can't you and father see that?"

"Believe me, I see it," Kemi chuckled. "You're like a wild stallion that won't be broken. But that worries me."

"Why?"

"Because wild stallions often find themselves in dangerous situations. Some of them come up lame or even die. I don't wish this for you."

"Sitting in my room won't keep me safe."

"No one said you had to sit in your room. But you don't have to chase danger either." She patted K'lani's hand. "Find the balance between the two. There you'll discover your true self."

Kemi always enjoyed studying philosophy. It's one of the reasons she and Valerios got along so well. K'lani did her share of studying as well but she preferred a life of adventure. The sisters were opposites of each other and yet their two halves made a whole.

K'lani offered an awkward hug, and they started a stroll back towards the palace together. As they walked, she slipped her tunic back on and tied off her hair in a tight bun. Her father was already angered, no sense increasing his rage with a sloppy appearance. But K'lani's own rage flared up as she saw Zhayn headed their way.

"Try not to be too hard on him," Kemi whispered. "He means well."

K'lani grunted. She had no intention of taking it easy on Zhayn. He didn't deserve her understanding after selling her out. K'lani readied herself for a fiery discussion only Zhayn came with more pressing matters.

"Emperor Kazu needs you both now," he said. "The council is gathering. There's trouble coming."

His face sat like stone. This was no joke. At the mention of the word "trouble," K'lani's hand instinctively fell upon the dragon blade dagger hidden at her back. She'd taken the impressive weapon from the dragonslayer herself. Clutching the hilt brought her comfort in times of distress. But something told her they were going to need more than a simple dagger to face the untold danger. Perhaps they would need the dragon warrior herself.

19

Savage Lands

Rayna needed K'lani. To find her meant going across the sea to Ischon. Ryu seemed excited for the trek. After what they encountered returning from Kartha, another voyage across the ocean didn't sit well with Rayna.

Still, she felt more at ease on the back of her dragon than traveling by ship. For one thing, Ryu could get to Ischon much faster than any other vessel. They needed to reach the city and find K'lani urgently. Not only that but Rayna also found she missed the girl's company.

Her innocence and naivety brought a lightness in the face of overwhelming danger. After the way she left things with Jagger, Rayna needed some levity. Leaving him behind brought a sense of loss that crept over her like a punch in the gut. Her stomach churned as Ryu flew over Pelanor Pass and out across the expanse of the eastern sea.

"You can slow down a little," she called. "Ischon isn't going anywhere."

Ryu chuffed at her then spread his wings fully to glide through the air. Rayna leaned forwards and patted his neck as a thank you. Shifting back to a seated position she caught motion from the corner of her eye. A flurry of black ropes came across the sky towards them. By the time she realized they were nets it became too late. She couldn't react in time, and they got caught.

Launched from an unseen force below, the nets took hold of both dragon and rider. Ryu tried to angle up at the last second, but he couldn't maneuver himself fast enough. The ropes were heavy, weighed down by steel ball bearings meant to drag the prey from the sky.

With Ryu's wings pinned under the net they began to fall. One of Rayna's greatest fears came to fruition, and she could do nothing to stop it. A gust of air whipped her blonde braids into her face. She shut her solitary eye and gritted her teeth for the impact of the ground. It didn't come.

Instead, the two of them came to an abrupt stop still tangled in the net. When she opened her eye, Rayna found they remained in a precarious position. Held within the massive net they were left to swing back and forth over a pit so deep it seemed to go on forever.

Ryu struggled and bit at the ropes but couldn't find

enough leverage to get free. Rayna didn't even try to escape. She watched the figures spilling out from the forest all around them and knew it would be to no avail. They were caught, by whom remained to be seen.

The figures shuffled out from dense patches of trees. Their movements were chaotic, not a uniform approach. By the look of them they weren't a royal militia but still a group of sorts. Each wore a similar loin cloth and carried a club as a weapon. They held thick musculature on short frames. Dark hair hung from their shoulders and grew coarser across their torsos and legs.

"Savages," Rayna whispered to Ryu.

She knew he wouldn't understand the meaning of the word, but she did. It meant they'd been brought down into the Savage Lands. It meant they were in trouble.

The savage army swarmed underneath the net to get a better look at their catch. They began a series of hoots and howls that caused the excitement to grow deep into the crowd. Angling her head as best she could, Rayna looked over the sea of the creatures. Not a female stood among them. Her hands clenched around the thick rope of the net as she realized why they grew so excited at the sight of her.

"We need to get out of here," she said aloud. "Burn them all."

"I can't."

Hearing Ryu speak stunned her more than the rough

fingers of the Savages poking at her thighs. She shifted away from their prodding and looked to her dragon. Mistaking her shock for confusion Ryu began to explain why he couldn't use his dragon's breath.

"If I try to ignite these little men in fire while we're caught up together, I could burn you as well."

"You can speak?"

He angled his head and chuffed. "I've been speaking. This is just the first time you understood me."

"How?"

"Perhaps the Source Magic is spreading across the land. Which means we need to get free of this trap before the entire world falls to it."

Before they could come up with a new plan, the Savages dragged Rayna from the net. Ryu tried to reach out for her with his claw but caught a dozen or so hits across his knuckles. The Savages continued to beat him back as they threw Rayna into the dirt.

Dozens of them pounced upon her holding down each limb while others took her weapons and tore at her clothes. She tried to scream only to have a gnarled hand cover her mouth. So many of them were atop her scrambling for position that she started to suffocate. She couldn't speak, couldn't move, and now she couldn't breathe. Rayna was at their mercy as she heard Ryu growling and calling out for her.

Sharp nails tore at her breasts and pulled apart her

thighs. She tried to will away the atrocity that was about to happen to her. If Source Magic did spill over the land maybe she could tap into it. Magic didn't come, a Source God did.

"Stop that, you ruffians!"

The voice called out with an ethereal echo booming off the everlasting sky. At the woman's order the Savages backed away from Rayna and bowed their heads. Free of their calloused hands she scrambled back into a tight ball trying to collect her wits and her weapons.

A dark beauty hovered over the Savages as they mewled like wounded animals. Adorned in deep set leathers she floated there on skeletal wings looking over the collective. Then her eyes shifted to Rayna. Naked, weaponless, she felt more vulnerable than ever before.

"Did they fowl you, child?"

Shaking, Rayna assessed herself. Then she shook her head. This seemed to please the goddess.

"Good. I provide these beasts with enough pleasure. You are meant to remain untouched for me."

"Leave her alone!"

Ryu's growling angered the goddess. "You would choose a mortal woman over the one that made you?"

"Rayna is more of a mother to me than any of you Source Gods," Ryu argued.

She laughed. "Except that Rayna's the one who killed your dragon mother in the first place."

Rayna knew the day would come when Ryu would learn the truth. In fact, she wondered if his memories of that day on the Graven Peaks would let him recall what happened. She didn't expect the gravity of the situation to reveal itself in the presence of a Source God.

Thealia, Goddess of the Earth, looked nothing like Rayna expected. She imagined a figure of jubilation that radiated with a healthy glow and nourishment from the land. Instead, the figure before her appeared malnourished. Dark hair with wisps of gray within circled her shoulders. A stripe of dust appeared painted across her eyes and down her chin. She wielded a scythe in withered hands while floating upon the large, skeletal wings.

Thealia looked used up as though her Source Magic were drying out. It gave Rayna hope for the battle ahead. As the goddess remained distracted with Ryu, she dressed and gathered her sword. The Savages caught sight of her advances and began to throw a fit. Their outburst caught Thealia's attention, and she shouted for silence.

Her words boomed off the sky as though the Savage Lands existed in a chamber. Rayna had to cover her ears as the vibrations rattled inside her head. When she regained her bearings, she came to find it wasn't a suggestion from Thealia but an insistence backed by a spell. All the Savages had gone silent and Ryu with them.

Though he tried to speak he no longer could.

For whatever reason, Thealia had spared Rayna the same indignity. She floated there waiting for Rayna's next move as though they were deep in a game of wits at the local tavern. Shaking off the last few moments, Rayna steadied her nerves and went to face the Goddess of Earth.

"You know I'm here to stop your rise to power, Thealia," she called. "I killed your siblings. I'll end you as well!"

Thealia set herself down upon the ground. Tucking her skeletal wings back she walked towards Rayna undaunted. Bhrytbyrn felt heavy in her hands and her palms grew slick with sweat as she held it. But Rayna was ready to do battle no matter the outcome. Besting the last two Source Gods gave her confidence in killing them all. Thealia didn't seem to care about her past accomplishments.

"They are not my kin, silly girl," she said, her voice continuing to echo as she spoke. "And I'm not going to fight you. That wouldn't be fair."

"Since when do the Source Gods concern themselves with what is fair?"

"I have no interest in the destruction of this world like the others do," she explained. "Every blade of grass, every tree, and every animal came of my creation."

Her eyes fell on Ryu as she spoke of her creations. Back

in the day when the world was fresh and new the Source Gods populated the land with magical creatures. Only in the wake of the human uprising did they start to wane. Many went extinct.

That didn't keep the gods from claiming them as their toys. The Goddess of Earth went one step further. She claimed them as her children. It seemed she wanted them returned to her. Rayna had a problem with that.

Even in the wake of the tragic death of Ryu's mother Saarath becoming known that didn't change matters. Rayna was his rightful guardian. No one was going to change that, not even a goddess.

"You can't have Ryu."

"I don't want the dragon, I want you!" Thealia exclaimed. "I'll repopulate the world based in your image of beauty and strength."

"How? As a plaything for your monsters?"

"A simple sacrifice. Don't think of it as death. You'll be the catalyst for a new creation."

"And if I refuse?"

Thealia's lips twisted. "Then I'll kill you."

"Doesn't seem like much of a choice. You're going to kill me either way."

"My way spares your dragon and your friends. It makes you a martyr for a glorious purpose."

Rayna hefted Bhrytbyrn overhead. "I never did care for glory."

"Pity."

She waited for Thealia to engage but, like the Goddess of the Sea, her puppets led the attack instead. The Savages charged forwards as Thealia lifted on broken wings to watch the carnage. A quick pass of her palm over the dragoneye brought fire to blade. It was enough to keep a wide arc between herself and the frenetic mob.

Pressing them back with the blade of fire gave her opportunity. The Savages moved one by one rather than in a mass attack. This let Rayna cut them down strategically. But Rayna needed to keep up her energy. If she faltered just once the horde would break through her defenses and overpower her.

Only a few fell before her arms grew tired. They were pushing her further back towards the massive pit. Noting her surroundings, Rayna let them drive her back. When she was close enough it gave her the chance to strike the net that still held Ryu. Bhrytbyrn cut through the ropes as though they were silk threads.

He burst from the trap and hung on the air for a moment. Rayna feared his need for revenge would be conducted against her. Instead, he turned his attentions on Thealia barreling into her like an arrow. They each spread their wings and battled high in the air until Rayna could no longer see them.

Taking her attention off the Savages for even a moment led to an all-out assault. Noting the fire blade turned the opposite way gave them a chance to charge in. Rayna spun back around just before they clipped her legs from beneath her. She hopped back from the tackle causing several of the Savages to plummet into the pit behind her.

More came charging in without fear of the fire. They clubbed Rayna in the head, shoulders, and arms until she fell to her knees. Still clutching her broadsword, she countered the attacks as best she could. But the numbers were growing too large. Soon they would overtake her.

Remembering their intent from before, Rayna opted for another way out. She threw herself into the pit out of their reach. The fall went on for what seemed like an eternity. As she fell, she worked. Taking the whip of bones from her belt she wrapped it around the hilt of her sword. With an overhead toss she launched the blade at the wall.

The tip pierced through the stone and lodged itself there. Rayna held tight to the whip as her momentum shifted and she struck the wall shoulder first. The impact caused her grip to slip but she regained control.

Dangling over the nothingness of the chasm she started to pull herself up. Overhead a massive blast of flame carried across the opening of the pit. She heard screaming from above and several of the Savages fell past her with limbs ablaze. One of the falling bodies narrowly missed landing atop her. Rayna had to swing and sway out of the way of the carnage until it finally ceased.

She called out for Ryu hoping he could hear her way down below. When he didn't respond right away, she wondered if he lost his fight with Thealia. Rayna struggled to climb up out of the chasm. It was several feet high before she could reach the edge. Her arms ached from the battle with the Savages. She felt a pain in her finger as though it may be dislocated or fractured. It made holding onto the whip impossible. She fell.

Miles down and she still hadn't hit the bottom. Rayna wondered if it were a bottomless pit or else, she may wake in the underneath where the Source Gods dwelled for so many centuries. Finally, she came to a stop. Her body landed atop a familiar set of scales as Ryu swept down and caught her. Rayna held tight to him as he flew straight up out of the hole.

Back on solid ground Rayna lamented her weapons remained stuck in the chasm wall. Ryu huffed plumes of heavy smoke from his nostrils that almost singed her hair. Then he went down and retrieved Bhrytbyrn and the whip for her.

"Thank you, my friend, for everything," she told him.

He nodded. She hoped he would speak but Thealia's spell still held. Remembering the Goddess of Earth and her powers, Rayna readied herself for a battle. But it seemed Thealia was no more. Nothing but bodies, dust, and broken wings littered the ground where they stood.

Ryu had won this war for them.

"Returned to the earth from whence she came," Rayna said.

She needed a moment to regroup. Her burden didn't become any less heavy with the fall of each god. The challenges grew harder each time. Rayna only hoped that K'lani still held favor with Cebrios, the God of Wind. Then maybe the final Source God would listen to reason rather than striking first.

20
Kiss of the Dragon

K'lani sat on the steps of the palace with Zhayn next to her. His legs were much longer than hers and stretched down the second step. She stared at his feet as he wiggled his toes inside his sandals.

"What're you looking at?" he asked.

"Your feet are too small for your body."

"The war room is preparing for a battle with the Source Gods and you're talking about my feet?"

"I'm sorry, I'm nervous," she admitted. "When I get nervous, I blurt out random facts."

He wrapped his arm around her shoulders and pulled her close to him. His comforting touch was sudden, and it made K'lani tense up. Zhayn didn't notice. He simply rubbed her shoulders and tried to calm her down.

"It's going to be alright."

She pushed his arm off. "How can it be alright? The

Source Gods are angry with us!"

"We'll figure it out."

"Source Gods!" she repeated. "They are the Creators. We're not going to figure anything out. Whatever they wish to happen will happen."

"Emperor Kazu has a plan."

She could see that Zhayn wanted to believe her father held all the answers. Truth was Kivu Kazu had used up his share of favors with the Gods. If Ischon embraced the reality of the situation at hand, they would all be screaming in the streets. Better to bide their time with false hope. That is what the kingdom had come to: lies.

But K'lani didn't want to let any of this on to Zhayn. Let him have his false belief if it made him feel better. When the time came, he would learn the truth. By then, K'lani would've formulated her own plan.

She studied the Source Gods long enough to know each of them held a weakness. That is why they were better off working as a single unit. If the four of them broke off on their own, each of them vying for position as the new ruler, then they could be defeated. The secret lay in their egos.

As they sat there the sky above began to turn. It churned in purple and orange until settling into a blue-black darkness. Thick, gray clouds blotted out the sun causing the day to drop into an unnatural night.

"A storm is rolling in," Zhayn said looking up.

"That's no storm," K'lani told him. "The God of Wind is coming."

"How can you tell?"

They stood together and K'lani pointed out at the expanse of the sky. Far off in the distance a figure appeared within the clouds. It was large with a wingspan that could blot out the sun. The figure drew closer with an unimaginable speed.

While K'lani and Zhayn stood in awe watching, the doors opened behind them and soldier poured out by the dozen. Archers lined the towers, men on horseback took to the grounds, and finally the Wind Raiders came.

On Ischon, they held one of the greatest defense measures of any kingdom before them. The Aruda, king of all birds, with brilliant golden feathers and large enough to carry a grown man. They could fly faster than the wind itself. In service to the empire of Ischon, the Aruda kept the island safe from intruders. Now, they were called to battle their creator: Cebrios, God of Wind.

Zhayn took K'lani's hand and held her back out of harm's way. She looked on as the golden wings streaked overhead. They held no fear going straight towards their enemy. K'lani longed to be one of them. A soldier on the battle front protecting her city and her people.

She watched as they encircled the shadowy figure. Using formations learned over a thousand years, the Wind Raiders engaged the intruder to a degree that he

became overwhelmed and had to set down on the
ground. That's when the Khai took over. They rode in on
horseback ready for a fight. But as they got closer,
screams pierced the air. Many of them turned around
and started to ride back towards the castle.

K'lani pulled free of Zhayn and started to sprint out
towards the chaos. He tried to hold her back but once
she slipped from his grip, he followed close behind her.
They ran past the Khai riders who held terror on their
faces. K'lani drew her dragon blade dagger; Zhayn a
short sword gifted by his father. The two of them
prepared to fight though they didn't know what they
were facing. When they reached the summit, K'lani no
longer wanted to engage.

The Khai riders who remained had surrounded the
intruder and were holding her back with spears. Above,
the Aruda continued to circle in case the red dragon
decided to ascend. When K'lani saw Rayna and Ryu
there on Ischon she thought it must be a dream. But
when Bhrytbyrn lit up in Rayna's hands, she knew it to
be true. Then the grave reality of the situation dawned
on her.

"Rayna, put it down!" she called. "The archers will kill
you!"

Rayna used the blade to keep the Khai at bay. Ryu also
used intimidation rather than force to drive the soldiers
back. Had they meant for war, the two of them could've

obliterated the entire force by now. But K'lani knew otherwise. Rayna was a friend.

Again, she called for a truce. "Rayna, please."

Finally, Rayna saw her and smiled. But she still didn't put down her sword.

"Tell them to back off first," she said.

"You know this woman?" Zhayn asked.

"She's a friend," K'lani told him. Then she pushed through the soldiers and tried to keep order. "Step back, give her space."

The Khai didn't listen. They had their orders from Captain Khadan. Nothing the emperor's daughter said would change their minds. The massive dragon had some of them turning away. Perhaps Ryu would help rally K'lani's cause.

"If you don't step back the dragon will burn you."

"Don't tell them that!" Rayna called. "We come in peace."

"Prove it." Zhayn had pushed through the pack and come up to K'lani's side. "Lower your weapons and the Khai will do the same."

Rayna hesitated. She looked between K'lani and Zhayn then finally agreed to terms. Dousing the flame, she sheathed Bhrytbyrn and slipped off Ryu's back. The moment her feet touched the ground K'lani embraced her.

"I thought you were dead."

"Felt like I was for a time," Rayna whispered.

Zhayn stepped forward then. He spoke as the diplomatic heir he'd been groomed to become. K'lani preferred the carefree young man she'd grown up with.

"If you'll follow me to the castle. Emperor Kivu Kazu should like to speak with you." He paused and looked over at Ryu. "You can leave your dragon here."

Rayna's one good eye narrowed as she looked Zhayn over. She was assessing him and the merit of his words. K'lani had seen her do it before. Rayna held a keen ability to sense danger. Still uncertain of Zhayn's motives, she glanced at K'lani who nodded in approval.

"Very well," Rayna told him. "My dragon will stay behind but know that if anyone approaches with malicious intent, he will defend himself."

"You need not worry about that," Zhayn replied. "We have a great reverence for dragons on Ischon."

Rayna patted Ryu's neck then motioned for Zhayn to lead the way. The three of them joined the Khai and rode back towards the castle. K'lani couldn't stop smiling at Rayna as they traveled.

"Stop staring at me." Rayna's gruff attitude only made K'lani smile more.

"I can't help it," she said. "I'm just so happy to see you."

"I'm happy to see you as well but this isn't a joyous reunion." Rayna furrowed her brow. "There's trouble afoot."

"The Source Gods."

"You know?"

"Yes, we thought you were Cebrios, God of Wind, come to reclaim the gifts he bestowed on us," K'lani explained. "That's why they greeted you with such aggression."

"I understand. And I'm pleased you're already caught up with the problem at hand. I'll need your help to put an end to it."

"Me?" K'lani grew surprised. "No, you'll want to speak with my father, the emperor. He'll be the one who can help."

~

"Absolutely not!" Emperor Kazu shouted. "We will not take up arms alongside a ruffian from Atharia."

Rayna's welcome to Ischon rivaled her unpleasant stay on Kartha. It seemed the emperor did not like dealing with outsiders. When K'lani tried to vouch for Rayna, this angered him even more. He blamed Rayna for wooing his young daughter away. For such a small man he held a large temper and an even bigger imagination.

The expanse of the imperial throne almost enveloped Emperor Kazu. It sat high upon a rectangular stage in the center of the throne room. The throne itself seemed simple in design. Angled slats of dark wood and a single cushion on the seat. Built over the top of it was a lacquered cypress wood structure imbued with golden statues that depicted their war birds.

Emperor Kazu took his formal seat while next to him, beneath a smaller structure, a young woman sat upon her own throne. She held similar features to K'lani though much more delicate. Her green eyes kept watch on Rayna since they entered the throne room.

Kazu, dressed in green robes flecked with gold and carrying a wooden scepter, continued to shout down at Rayna. Many times, he mixed up his tongues and spoke with the ancient language of Ischon. Finally, Rayna raised her hand to interrupt him. This pulled a gasp from the onlookers as though she insulted their emperor. She didn't care.

"Sir, we don't have time for any of this. The God of Wind is coming, and he will not be reasoned with, or bargained with. I've tried that with the other Source Gods. He will not stop until all of us are dead."

As if triggered by something Rayna said, the young girl watching her finally spoke up. Her voice matched her features with a softness that rivaled fine crystal.

"You've killed the other Source Gods?"

"Yes," Rayna told her.

The girl stood. "Then you are the mighty slayer."

"That's what I've been trying to tell you, Kemi. This is Rayna the dragonslay...." K'lani said, then corrected herself. "This is Rayna the dragon warrior."

The girl, Kemi, descended the steps and came to face Rayna. She smelled of honey and even up close her voice seemed like a whisper in the wind.

"You fought side-by-side with Valerios."

"I did."

"He was to be my husband."

It all came rushing back to Rayna then. The way Valerios used to speak of his Kemi across the sea. How he longed to return to her and marry as they planned. That would never be. Valerios fell in battle betrayed by a friend. Kemi didn't need to know any of that.

"He was a good man, and he died a hero defending me." Rayna bowed her head as she spoke.

Kemi smiled and touched Rayna's cheek. "K'lani has told me what happened. I don't blame you, Rayna. Please don't blame yourself. Valerios is at peace now. My sister helped escort his spirit to the other side. He sits with my mother now. I shall see him again someday."

"That's enough," Emperor Kazu said. "You've already spoiled one of my daughters. You won't have Kemi as well."

To this Rayna couldn't help but laugh. "If I wanted your daughters, sir, I would have them. But I'm not here for them; I've come to stop the God of Wind. If you won't help me, I'll be on my way."

"Father, please," Kemi said. "Valerios trusted her. Why

can't you?"

"Very well," Kazu replied. "K'lani will show the dragon warrior to her quarters. We'll discuss plans on how to approach the Source God problem in the morning."

The emperor may have been persuaded by his daughter, but a tension still hung in the air. Rayna wanted nothing more than to finish dealing with the Source Gods and move on. She still had a quest to complete. Rayna made a promise to bring Ryu to the Isle of Dragons and she intended to keep it.

"Do you think Ryu wants to go?" K'lani asked as she guided Rayna to her sleeping quarters.

"I'm not sure but I can ask him." She grinned at K'lani. "He speaks now."

She seemed unfazed by the revelation. "He's always spoken."

"He never spoke to me before." Rayna frowned. "And he hasn't spoken since we left the Savage Lands."

"Maybe he's angry with you."

K'lani motioned her inside the room. Rayna expected a lavish setup with a private bath, ornate bed, and dressing gowns spun of silk. Instead, the room held a single sleeping mat upon the floor and a washing basin. One solitary window offered small streaks of sunlight. As it waned, an oil lantern would be used as a source of light.

For a moment Rayna thought she might be held prisoner until she realized that only royalty was offered the finer things on Ischon. She was an unwanted guest, so they gave her a soldier's sleeping quarters.

"I wouldn't be surprised if Ryu is mad at me," Rayna continued the conversation pretending to be undisturbed by her sleeping arrangements. "There's a lot of that going around."

"Jagger?" K'lani asked as though she sensed Rayna's distress.

"Yes. We left on bad terms."

"He seemed angered the last time I saw him."

"It's more than that now. I don't know if he'll ever forgive me for the things that happened."

"If it's any consolation, I'm not mad at you."

"It helps, thank you."

With swift, unexpected movements, K'lani leaned in and kissed Rayna. Her lips were soft enough, but nothing sparked inside Rayna the way it did when she kissed Jagger. Pressing her lips to his stirred her entire body.

K'lani pulled away and caught Rayna's expression of shock. It caused her cheeks to flush pink in embarrassment. She started to sputter an apology, but Rayna waved it off.

"That was nice but let's not cross that line, alright?"

The girl nodded though she seemed disappointed with

Rayna's response. She had unrequited love interests before but never a friend. Things felt awkward between them now. Rayna tried to change direction and lead K'lani down a different path.

"Besides, what about that young man you were with?"

"Zhayn?" K'lani said his name in both disgust and reverence.

"Yes, him. He seemed to like you."

"We grew up together. He's like my brother. It would be weird to think otherwise."

"You'd be surprised. That's how Jagger and I started as well." Rayna showed off the ink embedded in her arm to stifle the girl's infatuation. "Now we're promised to each other."

"I see."

"It's late. We should all get some rest. Matters of the heart can wait."

"You're right. Sleep well."

As K'lani departed, Rayna tried to leave her with uplifting words. "We traveled to Ischon to seek your aide, not Emperor Kazu's. You have more skill than you realize."

"And you're a lot kinder than you like to let on." K'lani flashed a smile. "Good kisser too."

They continued chatting for a while more. Each filled the other in on their days since splitting up at Mako. It was a nice reunion but one that needed to be cut short as the pull of exhaustion weighed on Rayna. K'lani returned to her own quarters while Rayna tried to get some rest.

She settled down on the sleeping mat. It was thin and didn't provide much support, but Rayna slept on worse before. Besides, her body was weary from the battle with the Savages. With the late hour at hand, she expected to drift off into a sound sleep. But it was her mind that needed calming. It continued to race throughout the night. Thoughts of past grievances plagued her sleep. Finally, she got up and began to wander the grounds.

The hum of a flute caught her attention, and she followed the sound until she found the source. Zhayn was sitting outside upon the steps playing different melodies on a hand-carved, wooden flute. Next to him a sack of herbs caught Rayna's attention.

Ischon was known for its herbal remedies. One of the most popular among traders was the ashwa. It helped to ease the mind of anxious thoughts and relax the body of pain. Rayna indulged in her share of imitations but after Valerios introduced her to the purity of the ashwa she couldn't go back.

Zhayn glanced up as she drew nearer. He didn't seem as concerned about her presence as the emperor had been. She motioned to sit, and he gave a nod. Then he returned to playing.

"That's a lovely melody," Rayna told him.

"It's a hymn I learned as a child," he replied. "It calms my spirit when I play it."

"You're a wild one, are you?"

"No, I'm usually at peace but right now it's bucking like a wild horse."

"Hence the ashwa."

At his confused look, Rayna pointed towards the sack. He picked it up and gave a laugh.

"I forgot that was there," he said.

"Maybe you've had too much already."

He shook his head. "I don't indulge. This is for Kemi."

"Kemi?" Rayna was surprised. "She doesn't seem the sort to take any intoxicants."

"Normally she doesn't," Zhayn explained. "But she hasn't been sleeping well since learning of Valerios' death."

"I can understand that. His death still haunts me as well."

"Is that why you're still awake?"

"No, other things plague my thoughts."

Zhayn passed the aswha to her. "Please, help yourself."

Rayna thanked him then took to preparing the smoke. She leaned back against the steps and inhaled awaiting that sense of relief to come. Instead, the ashwa made her stomach churn and she began a fit of coughs. Zhayn reached over and patted her back until the smoke cleared her lungs.

"Not used to the purity?"

Rayna tamped out the ashwa in disappointment. "That doesn't usually happen. Are you sure that's genuine ashwa?"

"I picked it myself."

"Maybe my body is spent from all the travel." She looked away in embarrassment. "I don't like heights. That makes flying on the back of a dragon a source of anxiety for me."

"Makes sense," Zhayn agreed. "I didn't like riding the Aruda at first. But you get used to it."

"You're a soldier then?"

"No, I'm meant to take over my father's seat at the council. But I believe any man dealing in the politics of the nation should know the ways of the warrior."

"That's smart. I've known many rulers who sit back and let their soldiers go to war without ever lifting a weapon themselves. It was the catalyst to their downfall."

"Things on Ischon are done differently. But with the God of Wind coming, we're going to need every able-bodied man, woman, and child in our ranks to help defend the palace. Which is why I'm glad you're here, dragon warrior."

"I'll do what I can."

"Are you and K'lani sleeping together?"

Rayna had started back inside when Zhayn asked the

unsettling question. She rejoined him on the steps where she showed the inked brand upon her arm. It caught him by surprise until she explained.

"I'm bound to another back on Atharia," she said. "K'lani has become a good friend, nothing more."

"I appreciate your candor. It's not really my place to ask but, like you said, certain thoughts plagued my mind keeping me from sleep."

"Is it because you care for her?"

"Of course. I've known K'lani since we were small children."

Rayna patted him on the shoulder. "Take good care of her, Zhayn."

He smiled back at her as she left. Walking back towards her sleeping quarters, Rayna had to pause in her steps. Her head spun and her stomach churned. She leaned against a marble pillar waiting for the sensations to ease. Something wasn't right though she couldn't discern the problem. There was no time to seek a healer either. Whatever troubled her would have to be pushed aside until after they dealt with the God of Wind.

She made it back to her room just in time. As she pushed open the door the unsettling in her stomach made her retch. After cleaning herself up she went to the small window and tried to get fresh air to her face.

Outside in the distance she spotted Ryu laying in the grass. His head rose as he spotted her. She gave him a wave and motioned for him to return to rest. Rayna wondered if he'd forgiven her for past transgressions. Had Jagger? Too many apologies to sort through. Her racing thoughts kept her awake until the break of dawn.

She readied herself for war. Sleep would come when she was dead. For now, the last of the Source Gods needed to be dealt with. But how would they defeat one who controlled the very air they breathed? She hoped their war room council held the answers.

21
These Dreams

K'lani's dreams were both dangerous and arousing. She found herself as the new ruler of Ischon. Her throne sat upon the large wooden dais bejeweled in greens and golds. Wind pulled at her hair sending it cascading around her shoulders like a cloak.

Everyone catered to her whims. Whatever she wished became reality. The palace danced, ate, and drank all in her honor. In the sea of faces she saw all her loved ones partaking in the festivities. Rayna was there and Kemi. Her father wore a smile for the first time in years. She even caught a glimpse of her mother though she couldn't quite make out her face in the crowd.

Then Zhayn approached out of nowhere. He wore multiple robes contrasting both light and dark. His long hair was pulled back atop his head highlighting his strong features. He bowed then reached his hand to her. She accepted and allowed him to lead her to the dance floor.

The rest of the crowd moved back as the two of them became the central focus. Zhayn moved her around in ways she never expected. He lifted her, spun her, and dipped her so far back she grazed the floor with her fingertips. Then he pulled her close, but it was no longer Zhayn who held her.

This man's hair was stark white with crystal blue eyes set against pale, almost translucent skin. He wore a short black robe fashioned at the waist with a thin belt. Gray fur covered his boots and the gauntlets at his wrists.

Despite his cool complexion he flashed a warm smile at K'lani. They continued to dance even as the crowd began to dissipate. The room spun round and round until it no longer remained. Gone were the party goers replaced instead by twinkling stars in the night sky. The floor beneath them had become thick clouds that cradled their feet with each step.

K'lani continued to embrace her dream and the man who shared it. She took in his exquisite features and their surroundings. It didn't take long to realize who invaded her fantasy.

"God of Wind," she whispered.

"You may call me Cebrios," he replied.

"Why have you come?"

"I always come when you call. Your faith is stronger than any who've come before you, K'lani."

"And yet now it wanes."

"Because the warrior woman and others tell you I have malicious intent?"

"The Source Gods will rise and turn back the sands of time to undo creation itself," K'lani said. "It's written in texts. Philosophers and seers foretold of this moment."

"Charlatans and tricksters, nothing more," Cebrios replied. "I've only come in answer to your prayers. The others had their own agenda."

"What prayers?"

"This one."

He waved his hand, and they were back in the throne room. K'lani sat upon her father's chair with Cebrios by her side. Below, the Khai soldiers knelt before her awaiting commands. She was respected and admired by all.

"You no longer must ask permission. You give the orders," Cebrios told her. "With that type of power, you could change the world. And isn't that everything you ever dreamed?"

"The orders are to fight you."

"Only if you deem it so."

He rose from his chair and circled around to face her. His eyes were captivating as they locked with her own and drew her into Cebrios' every word. K'lani leaned on the edge of her chair as he spoke with eloquence.

"Whatever you so desire all you need do is ask."

"And you will answer?"

"Have I ever let you down before?"

She shook her head. He spoke the truth. Many times she sought assistance from the God of Wind and he always responded. Rayna often spoke of how the Source Gods had forsaken her, but she did not believe the way K'lani did.

They revered Cebrios on Ischon. He wouldn't attack such loyal followers. What her father and the others believed to be the best approach was wrong. She could see that clearly now.

"When you wake, seek me."

Cebrios leaned in and kissed her. His touch bathed her in a peace she'd never known. She felt lighter than air as though floating on a cloud somewhere. When she woke the feelings stayed with her. She thought about telling Kemi or Zhayn what happened except they wouldn't listen. Their loyalty lay with Emperor Kazu and his words were law.

But Rayna didn't bend or bow for any ruler. She followed her own rule. When K'lani told her that Cebrios meant no harm to Ischon they could come up with an alternative plan together. Just like on Atharia they would be a team. If that meant going against her father's order, so be it.

22
Game of the Gods

Rayna felt lightheaded and nauseous. She wondered if the air on Ischon was too thin compared to Atharia. Elevation sickness plagued her before on the Graven Peaks. Perhaps her affliction with heights twisted into something more.

For an island known for its unity with the wind god they should have clearer air than any other land. That is, unless Cebrios was drawing it back and slowly suffocating the people. Rayna wouldn't be surprised. The games that the Source Gods played were often at the expense of humanity.

Still unable to get a full night's sleep, she left the palace grounds early. Only the men tilling the land were awake at that time. They pointed her towards a small stream where she may find some relief from the coolness of the water.

Not being cooped up in the small room helped clear her head. The fresh air also helped calm the rumbling of her stomach. Even with the strange, dark clouds moving across the sky it still felt pleasant on Ischon.

The island was a stark contrast to Kartha or even Atharia. There was beauty all around in the brightness of the fields or the rich colors on the mountains. The Source Gods took their time creating Ischon and the people there made certain to keep it beautiful. For all his faults, Emperor Kazu kept it safe as well.

Having a well-trained militia like the Khai soldiers and the Wind Raiders at your call helped deter intruders. No pirate or warlord would dare try to invade the land knowing they'd have to face those odds. But to a Source God, they were nothing but toys to bend and break as he chose.

After washing up, Rayna sought K'lani. She needed the girl's wisdom on the God of Wind. Surely, Cebrios had a weakness the same as his counterparts did. Together, they would find it and exploit it until he was conquered.

When she located K'lani, the girl was in higher spirits than the previous night. At first, Rayna equated her frenetic energy to preparing for the battle ahead. But stepping up to the chamber door she noticed a mania driving K'lani's actions.

She tore about the room gathering items at random and muttering to herself. It almost appeared as though she spoke incantations. Rayna had seen this type of energy before, but she couldn't quite recall where. K'lani had always been a bit of a mystery. Rayna learned on Atharia that sometimes it was better not to question her antics. Though now she didn't seem quite like herself.

Rayna moved deeper inside the room and K'lani still didn't notice her. She had taken to scribbling notes in a small booklet which kept her full attention. Rayna set her hand on K'lani's shoulder and gently nudged her. She glanced up for a moment then returned to her writings. Only after she'd finished scrawling what looked like gibberish did she jump up. Her frantic movements almost caused the two to knock heads.

"Rayna, I'm so glad you're here!"

A smile crept across Rayna's face as she remembered chatting with Zhayn the previous night. She glanced at K'lani's bed which still had its coverings in disarray. Now she started to put the pieces together.

"Did you have a good night?" Rayna asked in jest awaiting K'lani's recount of her passionate night.

"The best!"

Her excitement was infectious. Rayna sat at the edge of the bed and allowed K'lani to tell her tale. They could spare enough time for the girl to share an enjoyable memory before they went into battle with the God of Wind.

"Did a special man pay you a visit?"

"Indeed, he did."

Rayna chuckled. "Zhayn was asking about you last night. I'm glad to hear he had the balls to make a move."

To this, K'lani crooked her head. She stared at Rayna as though she were speaking in tongues. The story she had to tell didn't include the handsome, young warrior. 'Twas the God of Wind that came calling, invading K'lani's dreams like a chaos spirit.

"Cebrios came to me," K'lani explained. "He spoke of proffering peace with the kingdom."

Rayna grew uneasy. "Exactly what were his terms?"

"He didn't have any. I'm going to speak with my father on his behalf."

"Why you?"

"I'm his delegate." A maddening grin spread her lips wide. "Together we're going to change the world."

The crazed look in her eye, and the way she spoke with such a rapid pace, jarred Rayna's memory. Now she remembered where she'd seen this type of energy before.

Back when Toth chased the rush of growing magic he started to sound like a madman. Nothing could sway him from what ultimately burned him alive and led to his rise as the God of Fire. Now, K'lani held that same energy. Rayna hoped it wasn't too late to pull her back from the abyss. She measured her words and spoke with care so as not to cause an emotional eruption.

"Source Gods lie."

Rather than go off on a rant, K'lani tried to reassure Rayna. "I know you've had your difficulties with the other gods, but Cebrios is different."

"You must trust me, K'lani. He's using you as a pawn in a game."

Now the emotions came flooding over the girl like a torrential storm. K'lani often expressed her admiration and loyalty to the God of Wind. But something swayed her into absolute obsession.

Like Toth, she wouldn't hear any words spoken against Cebrios no matter how damming. Instead of being open and listening to an alternative viewpoint, K'lani verbally attacked her friend.

"I knew my father and the others would be stubborn, but I expected you to understand."

"I do understand. I understand that he's manipulated you with false hope."

"You're wrong, Rayna. And I'm going to prove it to you!"

K'lani tried to barge out of the room. When Rayna caught her arm to keep her from doing anything foolish, she reacted with violence. A quick, open-palm strike caught Rayna across the bridge of the nose sending her stumbling backwards.

The blow had much more behind it than simple, physical force. K'lani was too small and too unskilled to knock Rayna back in such a way. She remembered their time on Atharia when an extra gust of wind would propel K'lani up into the air or out across the sea.

At times, if the God of Wind allowed it, she could even fly. Cebrios controlled her actions and compelled her to think in ways that mirrored his own. If Rayna couldn't pull K'lani back from the brink Emperor Kazu may have to kill his own daughter.

23
God of Wind & Warfare

K'lani didn't know where she was running off to, only that she needed to get away from Rayna. Her bias towards magic clouded her good judgement. Cebrios promised peace but Rayna's nature always sought war. It was why she kept running into battle on Atharia. If not for Rayna's incessant need to fight, then Valerios would still be alive.

Hurrying from the palace she ran into Zhayn just outside the gates. He was headed towards the training area to join the Khai soldiers. When he spotted K'lani rushing by he tried to stop her. Zhayn always tried to stop her. He was another one impeding K'lani's wants.

She thirsted for more than just being the emperor's second daughter, but no one could see it. Only Cebrios embraced the future K'lani saw for herself. He knew the good she could do if given the proper chance. That's why she needed to get to him, and no one would stand in her way.

"Where are you going?" Zhayn asked.

"Away from here."

"K'lani, wait!" He reached out and took her hand. "What's wrong?"

She rubbed her temples trying to soothe a sudden ache there. "Everything is wrong."

"Let me help you."

"No, I have to go."

"I'll go with you."

"I said no!"

With that she shoved Zhayn back only she pushed too hard. A wind assault channeled through her palms, and it threw Zhayn five feet in the air. He came crashing down through a vendor table in the marketplace. Wood splintered across his body leaving cuts on his bare arms and face.

The marketplace erupted in panic. They shouted and scrambled for cover unsure of what attacked Zhayn. The shouting caught the attention of the Khai as they were marching towards the training fields. Captain Khadan ordered them towards the market to take up defensive positions.

As K'lani saw the Khai approaching she got scared. What had she done? Zhayn lay unconscious in the wreckage of the vendor stall. Her people ran around in fear and the soldiers were coming for her!

"Cebrios," she whispered. "Please help me."

"As you wish."

His words floated across the air and then he appeared out of nowhere. Wrapping an arm around her shoulders a sudden torrent of wind enveloped them both. As they lifted towards the sky, K'lani saw Rayna running out towards them.

~

She didn't make it in time. K'lani was already too high up when Rayna got to her. The God of Wind stood behind her with a grin on his face and the same glowing eyes she'd seen on the other Source Gods.

Cebrios was a tricky one. He didn't intend to fight them head on like Toth. And he wasn't interested in using warriors like Thealia and Persea. No, Cebrios preferred having a human shield. He looked for the most loyal of his followers and twisted her adoration for him. Having K'lani out front would keep the emperor at his mercy. Or so Rayna thought. But Emperor Kazu either didn't see his daughter up above or he didn't care.

He rushed outside with a pack of archers flanking him. Upon seeing the God of Wind, he gave an immediate order to shoot him down. The archers wasted no time in complying.

"Wait!" Rayna shouted. "He has K'lani up there."

Kazu looked at her for a moment. His face registered her words and then hardened again.

"It's for the greater good," he replied. Then he called for the order.

Rayna tried to stop the attack but there were too many archers firing all at once. The arrows moved in unison up towards the God of Wind. He stood safely behind K'lani. Once the arrows reached their target, they would only strike her. But Cebrios had other plans.

He spread his hands out causing a blast of air to push out across the field. The strength of the wind pushed back not only the arrows, but the archers as well. Everyone on the field was thrown backwards as though a hurricane swept through town.

Rayna tumbled head over shoulders until colliding with Zhayn's prone body. The young man remained unconscious on the ground. Rayna couldn't tell the extent of the damage he suffered nor the others who were thrown about. Reassessing herself she felt dizzy from the toss but managed to shake it off. When she looked back up to the sky, Cebrios and K'lani were gone. In their place a tremendous storm was brewing in the distance.

Emperor Kazu struggled to get up. Rayna took him under the arm and helped him to his feet. He no longer held the look of determination. She could see he was scared. As the wind grew fiercer, Rayna had to shout so

Kazu could hear her.

"Your god controls the weather?"

"Yes," he replied. "We pray to him to provide for our crops."

"He's not listening to your prayers any longer," Rayna told him. "And he has your daughter. We cannot move on him while she's in his control."

"I'm not going to let my kingdom fall," Kazu argued. "K'lani would understand."

He shook free of her grasp and started gathering his men. The stubborn old man cared more about his empire than his own children. It was the same way with all rulers that Rayna ever came across. If Kazu wouldn't listen to reason, then perhaps Kemi would.

24
Eye of the Storm

Kemi was nothing like her sister. She was raised as the doting daughter who followed her father's rule with no questions asked. K'lani was headstrong and curious. She questioned everything and did her own research to find suitable answers. But Cebrios' grip on her changed their roles. Now that K'lani followed the God of Wind blindly into battle, Kemi needed to step up and fight.

"I cannot," she told Rayna. "My father will manage this as he's always done in the past."

She was sitting in her room surrounded by trinkets sent to her by Valerios. It looked as though Kemi spent many hours lost in her past love. Nothing else seemed to matter to her, not even the safety of her sister or herself.

Rayna squatted down and turned Kemi to face her. She wanted her full attention as she related the grim future.

Instead, Rayna dug up the past. It was the only way to break Kemi's spell so together they could break the one K'lani was under.

"Valerios was not a man of action," Rayna told her. "He preferred to spend his time reading books and studying under many different masters."

"He was a thinker," Kemi said. "That's one of the reasons I fell in love with him."

"Except, when the time called for him to pick up a sword and fight, he didn't hesitate to do so," Rayna continued. "I don't expect you to go to war with us. But your voice is your sword. Use it to get your father to listen to reason. If you don't, not only will K'lani be lost but all of Ischon will fall."

~

When Cebrios swept her up she felt light and free. Watching her own father try to strike them down took away that sense of peace. When Cebrios pushed back the attack it made her smile. Damn them if they wouldn't listen. They would be conquered, and a new world order instituted.

Cebrios took her to the highest of peaks overlooking the expanse of Ishcon. No mortal could ever climb so high or breathe so freely in the thin air. But Cebrios welcomed K'lani into his world.

"Because you're special," he told her as though reading

her mind. "You are the one who is meant to rule."

"I wouldn't know where to begin," she admitted.

Cebrios wiggled his fingers and plucked an apple from an invisible tree then handed it to K'lani. When she bit into the skin, she tasted a sweetness that far surpassed anything she'd ever eaten. The apple was perfectly ripe and the freshness of it filled her with joy.

"It's as simple as that," Cebrios explained. "I willed the apple into existence and so it became. You could shape the world the same way."

"How? I have no powers."

Cebrios wiped the juice of the apple from her lips then glanced a kiss from them. K'lani stared up at him and smiled. His eyes entranced her like great crystal pools she wanted to wade deep into.

"You don't need to have powers," he told her. "You have me."

The surroundings changed to a spacious chamber beautifully dressed in colored draperies. A massive bed occupied much of the space covered in silks and thick furs. Cebrios lay K'lani down across the bed then stretched out beside her.

"Reality is what you wish it to be," he said, trailing a finger across the slope of her breast. "What do you wish?"

She parted her lips to speak and Cebrios caught them with his own. K'lani felt a sudden disorientation, a silver radiance dazzled her vision. The ground shifted beneath her as though they drifted on the everlasting sky. Cebrios took her there within the clouds setting the girl free and bringing to bare the woman K'lani always meant to be.

~

Rayna stood with Zhayn out on the balustrade that connected to K'lani's bed chamber. They watched as the sky above churned with colors. Flashes of light boomed within dark clouds, and they could hear the crack of thunder piercing the air.

"What's happening?" Zhayn asked aloud.

Rayna gave her best answer. "Nothing good."

Wherever Cebrios had taken K'lani he was continuing to poison her mind with empty promises. The Source Gods may have been creators back when they formed the world together but now, they sought destruction.

From her altercations with the others, she derived they held a great disdain for the humans who filled their land. The gods wanted to turn back the sands of time to when magic ruled. It was humans who hunted their magical creatures to gain power. Soon many of those creatures went extinct.

In their place stood those who sought power and pleasure above all. They poisoned the rivers, pillaged the land, and polluted the air. This angered the Source Gods until finally they woke with a mission to punish the people who inhabited their world.

For a long time, Rayna hunted dragons. She sought them for revenge not a need for power. Her anger was misplaced, and it caused a lot of harm to the species. That is what she saw in the Source Gods now. Their anger was misplaced. They sought to punish everyone rather than the few who put their wants above all else.

She had no luck trying to reason with Toth, Persea, and Thealia. By taking K'lani with him, Cebrios already declared war. He would not be reasoned or bargained with. They needed to make a stand against him.

Below in the courtyard Emperor Kavu's men were preparing for an all-out assault. They gathered the Khai soldiers along with every able-bodied man on Ischon to fight the God of Wind. They would lose.

"No matter how many men the emperor has in his army it won't do any good," Rayna said. "Magic needs to fight magic. I'm going to take Ryu and seek the God of Wind myself."

"That's a suicide mission," Zhayn told her.

"I see no other way."

Rayna leaned into the balustrade and looked down at the people preparing for war. Even from up high she sensed the fear coming from the farmers and armorers. Those who never stepped into battle before were being asked to face an impossible foe.

But they didn't ask questions or argue with the decree. Each man on Ischon was willing to give his life for the cause. Rayna didn't live on the island, and she owed no allegiance to its emperor. But she would give up her life for that of her friend.

Zhayn set a hand on her shoulder. "The Aruda are magical beings just like your dragon. You don't have to do this alone. I will join you."

"You're a good man, Zhayn."

"It's not about me," he replied. "It's about getting K'lani back."

Even after she'd thrown him through a wooden market cart, he still sought her safe return. Rayna admired his determination. She could tell by the look in his eye he would fly with her whether she wanted him to or not. Then a third joined their ranks.

Kemi sought them as the duo were packing up their respective winged beasts. As the son of a prominent figure inside the war council, Zhayn only needed ask and was granted a golden bird as his own. Rayna collected Ryu from the outskirts of town. They were filling saddle bags when Kemi came.

"I thought about what you said, and I want to help get my sister back."

Rayna gripped Kemi's hand grateful that she'd found her way clear to do the right thing. The three of them needed to slip away from the palace without alerting suspicion. Emperor Kazu would never agree to have his plans interfered with. Nor would he allow his eldest daughter to be put in harm's way.

Zhayn sat upon his war bird while Rayna climbed on Ryu's back. Once settled, she helped Kemi up behind her then they marched their winged companions out until the palace was no longer visible in the distance. Then they took to the sky.

"Hold on tight," Rayna told Kemi. "It can be a little overwhelming."

"You have a fear of heights," Kemi said.

"Yes," Rayna admitted, unsure how the princess knew such an embarrassing fact.

"Pressure points on the body can bring relief, may I show you?"

Skeptical of any such body work, Rayna still agreed to let Kemi try. She found the soft indentations at the back of Rayna's neck and applied firm pressure there. A wave of relief traveled down Rayna's neck and into the meat of her shoulders.

As Kemi moved her fingers in a circular motion, Rayna didn't even notice when Ryu lifted off the ground. Only when Kemi stopped the technique did Rayna realize they'd been flying long enough to gain great height.

"How do you feel?" Kemi asked.

"I must admit, that helped," Rayna told her.

"The same technique can subdue any nausea you may

feel."

"I'm feeling well enough now, thank you."

"Glad to hear it," Zhayn called from his war bird. "Now how do we find them?"

Rayna looked out across the expanse of the sky. The ebbing colors had waned and were replaced by an ongoing darkness. Even when the sun should be brightening up the day it did not appear. The only light they saw were thin streams of it cracking through the storm clouds. Rayna pointed in their direction.

"Seek the source."

Zhayn nodded agreement and they angled their flight towards the turbulence. Flying directly into the eye of the storm may seem reckless to the less experienced fighter. For Rayna, it was the only way.

25
Heroes & Monsters

K'lani thought bedding a god would make her wiser in some way. In fact, she felt no more enlightened than any other time she'd gone to bed with a suitor. Which was once on Atharia after drinking too much cheap mead.

After that tryst she felt dirty. Her union with Cebrios brought about questions. Were they lovers? Betrothed? On Ischon they took the physical act of love very seriously.

Once she dressed, K'lani sought Cebrios to have some of these concerns quelled. They moved position again; this time he stood out on a hilltop overlooking the city through a great mass of clouds. She wrapped her arms around his waist, and he pushed her off.

"They're coming."

Confused, K'lani followed his stare through the heavy

clouds and saw familiar faces headed their way. She expected that Rayna would seek her out. And it didn't surprise her that Zhayn would come for her as well. But seeing Kemi there made K'lani uncomfortable. She didn't want her sister to be in the line of fire.

"Perhaps they want to come to terms."

Cebrios didn't see it that way. He took K'lani's hand and pressed a dagger into her palm. It was her dragon dagger, the one Rayna gifted to her, but he'd infused it with power. The dagger almost seemed to come alive in her hand. She tried to give it back and Cebrios forced her to hold onto it.

"To refuse would be a mistake," he said. "They're coming to kill you. Defend yourself."

~

They flew endlessly, searching everywhere that the God of Wind may be hiding. Ryu and the Aruda were growing tired. They would have to set down soon and by then Emperor Kazu's army would be on the move.

One more pass and they would turn back. As they circled, Rayna noted the clouds ahead begin to part. They peeled back to reveal a hidden valley lush with tropical splendor. It was a direct contrast to the darkness that fell over Ischon.

Sweet-smelling flowers stretched across a bed of grass. The song of hidden birds floated out from the bushes. A great lake sat in the center filled by a waterfall that came from nowhere.

At the edge of the lake stood the God of Wind with K'lani at his side like a puppet on strings. She held the dragon dagger in one hand and clutched Cebrios' arm in the other. Rayna alternately seethed and ached looking at the scene.

When Ryu saw the dragon dagger he balked. His sudden movement startled the golden bird and they almost collided with each other. This brought a booming laugh from the wind god.

Rayna angled Ryu into an arc meant to circle around the back of Cebrios. But something unforeseen cut off their path. Ryu hit a wall that wasn't there causing him to spin out of control. This brought both Cebrios and K'lani to a fit of laughs. If not for Zhayn's quick action on the Aruda, the lot of them would've plummeted to their death.

Utilizing the bird's great talons, he caught hold of Ryu's long tail and helped stabilize the dragon. Noting the illusion that stood all around them, Rayna moved with extra caution as she instructed Ryu to land. Zhayn followed close behind but kept his golden bird aloft in case of more tricks.

"Too bad they didn't fall," K'lani said. "It would've made things easier."

"But not as much fun," Cebrios added.

Rayna stared at the girl as she dismounted from Ryu. She was different, angry. The light of hope that shined upon her face was replaced with deep creases of darkness. Strange how a Source God known for beauty could cause such ugliness.

This wasn't K'lani's true nature just as the waterfall behind them wasn't real. It reminded Rayna of their time back in the magic markets of Mako. She and Jagger had become infected with a spell that drew out all their innermost anger. They wound up insulting, and ultimately fighting each other until the spell was broken.

The only way to break the spell of a Source God that Rayna knew of was by countering it with something stronger. She reached up and helped Kemi down from Ryu. Rayna rested her hand on the hilt of Bhrytbyrn and the two of them approached. When they came too close, Cebrios halted them in their step by cracking open the ground on which they walked.

"That's far enough," he said.

"Very well, we can end things from right here," Rayna told him. Then to Kemi: "Your turn."

She nodded then called to her sister. "K'lani, please come home."

"I am home."

"No, you belong with me and father."

"Why? Neither of you ever wanted me there."

"That's not true."

Cebrios rolled his eyes. "Enough of the family reunion."

It was a trap just as Rayna expected. He drew them in close enough to dispense with them quickly. The pull of his hand dragged Kemi forwards until she was yanked into the cracked ground. Rayna dove onto her stomach and caught her arm just before the earth swallowed her whole.

Seeing this caused Zhayn to dive forwards on the golden bird. He charged the God of Wind without so much of a thought as to how powerful Cebrios was. It took seconds for him to pitch both man and bird into the lake and then seal it over in ice. Rayna continued holding onto Kemi, struggling to pull her back up. They were all in a precarious position and the God of Wind was just getting started.

~

K'lani stood by silently and watched as Cebrios assaulted her sister and Zhayn. Inside she screamed for him to stop. She couldn't reconcile her heart and head. Working towards the greater good meant getting all obstacles out of their way. But she couldn't ignore the ache her heart felt as she watched her loved ones in pain.

Rayna tried to pull Kemi up from a chasm that led to nowhere. Zhayn pounded on the sheet of ice keeping him trapped beneath the lake. Then it was Ryu's turn.

He came flying in towards Cebrios only to be blown back by winds that rivaled a tropical storm. K'lani watched helplessly as the dragon she'd come to love as her own was swallowed up by dark clouds.

Cebrios turned to her then. "It's your move."

He pointed to the dagger in her hands then motioned to Rayna. K'lani nodded knowing what needed to be done. She raised the dragon dagger high overhead. Rayna could've dropped Kemi into the chasm and defended herself. Instead, she just stared up at K'lani with her one blue eye. The other eye concealed by a patch that told a thousand tales.

It felt like wading through quicksand to get to that place in her mind which spoke the truth. But then only a matter of seconds to decide what she must do. A quick pivot on her feet and she turned the dagger into Cebrios' stomach. Using all the force she could, K'lani drove the dagger hard until the blade cut deep enough to disappear up to the hilt.

He howled and shook more from the betrayal of her attack than any pain. K'lani held on with both hands trying to drag the blade inside his body. His flesh tore away until it exposed sinew and a beating heart within the cavity of his chest.

It was blue like the color of his eyes which now held no center to them. They were mere pools of light like the sun's gaze. His handsome features hardened, and he stared at K'lani with such malice she feared he would bite her head clean off.

~

Rayna watched K'lani wake from the spell Cebrios held her under. She moved with quickness, aiming the dragon dagger at his heart but striking his middle instead. Still, Rayna held hope that the God of Wind would be weakened enough that they could finish him off together. Instead, the wound caused him to shift into a monstrosity.

The Source Gods were always depicted in writings as beautiful, ethereal creatures. From what Rayna saw, each of them was hideous in their own way. Cebrios just did a better job of hiding his true form. Until now.

Now, when faced with the betrayal of his underling, he let his inner beast out. Rayna dragged Kemi the rest of the way out of the chasm then withdrew her sword. She watched as Cebrios began to grow in height. He rose up until he reached the size of the imagined waterfall behind them. All the while K'lani held tight to the dagger plunged into his body.

Cebrios, now in true god form, plucked her from his chest and let her plummet to the ground below. Kemi cried out in terror as she watched her sister falling to her death. Rayna dropped her sword in a feeble attempt to catch the falling girl.

Before the two of them were splattered upon the grass, Ryu returned from beyond the clouds. He swooped in and caught K'lani just before impact. Behind him, a gathering of Wind Raiders came to join the fray.

The golden birds and their riders held no fear heading right for the God of Wind. He swatted them away like a horse chasing flies with its tail. Rayna watched in horror as they smashed against rock walls or crashed to the ground. Some of them fell upon the frozen lake causing it to crack enough for Zhayn to escape.

As the attacks on Cebrios continued, his illusions faded. There was no longer a cascading waterfall. The flowerbeds and lush grass became coarse sand. They did not float upon the clouds but stood upon the ground at the edge of the shore.

Zhayn crawled from the ocean not a frozen lake. He scrambled to Rayna's side and the two prepared to engage the God of Wind. He spotted them down below and tried to step on them. As he raised his massive leg, Ryu returned with K'lani on his back. She leaped from the dragon onto Cebrios taking him around the neck.

"Aim for his heart!" she screamed.

The two of them thrashed about as Cebrios tried to pull K'lani off his back. The distraction left his weakness exposed. Neither Rayna nor Zhayn carried a bow, but Rayna had another way.

Her very first dragon slain, Balorath, fell in a similar

manner. Rayna took a chance then and she would do the same now. Holding Bhrytbyrn overhead she tossed her sword like a spear. The strength of her body, honed by years of battle training, sent the blade across the air. It flew hard and fast towards Cebrios and found its mark in the soft, exposed tissue.

As the sword struck his heart, he arched backwards. The movement caused K'lani to lose her grip. She tumbled off but used her agility to roll over Cebrios' mighty shoulders. Falling past his chest, she caught hold of Bhrytbyrn's handle and ripped the sword free.

As the blade came loose it tore out the Source God's heart with it. This time as K'lani plummeted towards the ground both Rayna and Zhayn were there to break her fall. The same couldn't be said for the God of Wind.

Cebrios fell backwards like a tree torn from its roots. His massive body landed with a splash on the edge of the water. Strong tides, aggressive by the continuous storms, dragged the body into the ocean. The Source Gods had all returned from where they'd come.

~

In the days that followed K'lani tried to reconcile with what happened. She let herself become manipulated by a god and it almost cost her everything. Once the dust settled, and the casualties of war gathered, Emperor Kazu sequestered K'lani to her room. He made her stay locked inside like a prisoner for a full day.

Kemi snuck her food and Zhayn tried to keep her entertained through the locked door. After a while K'lani began to get stir crazy. She thought about trying to climb down from the balustrade to escape.

If she made it down it would take rushing out the gates, past the armed guards, and one-hundred feet from the palace before reaching safety. It didn't seem feasible. Besides, after almost losing everything at the hands of Cebrios, including her mind, K'lani embraced her home with newfound adoration. Whatever punishment her father saw fit for betraying her people, she would accept it.

When the time came to answer her crimes, she grew scared. A loud knock sounded out on the door. Each time the knuckles struck wood, K'lani felt it boom in her chest. Now was not the time to be overcome by emotion. She straightened up, wiped the tears from her eyes, and answered the door fully intending to accept her sentence.

K'lani expected to see Khai soldiers waiting on the other side of the door. Her father would make an example out of anyone who crossed his empire...including his own daughter. Instead, she saw a friendly face waiting when she opened it.

Rayna stood there with arms folded across her chest. She wore her full black and gold armor with Bhrytbyrn at her back. Multiple braids pulled back her blonde hair to expose her solitary eye. On the other side, a flowing mane cascaded over the eyepatch keeping it obscured from view. Even without the customary warpaint smeared across her eyes, Rayna looked ready for battle.

"They sent you to bring me?"

"I volunteered. Now let's go."

K'lani nodded and went willingly. She wasn't surprised to see Rayna there. Of all the people she'd wronged, Rayna was the worst of them. She sought K'lani's help and instead of offering it to her, they went to battle with each other.

If there were a way to take back her actions, she would do it no matter the cost. But not even the Source Gods could move time backwards. Now that they were all defeated, it was up to humanity to fend for themselves. That suited K'lani fine. She wondered how long the God of Wind had been using her for his own gain.

Every time she called out for his help, he manipulated her just a bit more until finally came the day when she fell to his charms completely. Bedding him seemed like a wonderful moment at the time. But once she realized the true monster lurking beneath his beautiful facade, it made her stomach churn to remember his touch.

Rayna escorted her down to the throne room without saying another word. Of all the things K'lani had done she hated that she broke their bond. It was hard enough getting Rayna to trust her in the beginning. Now that she betrayed her trust, K'lani knew there was no way of winning it back.

As expected, the throne room was packed with onlookers. Everyone from the royal council, members of the war room, Khai soldiers, and even staff filled the small space to see the traitor receive her punishment. Emperor Kazu sat on his throne with her sister Kemi occupying the smaller seat next to him. When he saw K'lani enter, he stood prompting everyone else in the hall to do the same.

Rayna walked K'lani in front of the emperor and then stepped off to the side. K'lani looked up into her father's stern face then glanced at her sister. She found no comfort in either of them. Only when she spotted Zhayn standing close by did K'lani feel somewhat at ease. He gave her a smile and a knowing wink as though to tell her things weren't all they appeared to be.

"Daughter, you have made questionable choices in your life," her father began. "No matter how much I tried to guide you on a path of peace you chose to walk in the boots of an adventurer. Because of this rebellious nature it left you susceptible to the God of Wind's manipulation. Seeing you take sides with him broke my heart."

"Father, I never meant to hurt...."

Kazu raised his hand as K'lani tried to speak her peace. She knew her words wouldn't be heard there, they never

were. But she at least wanted to try and defend her
actions though there was no excusing them.

"Let me finish," her father told her. "I was furious with
you and wanted nothing more than to see you punished
for your actions. But after much internal searching, and
hearing complementary words from the Atharian
woman, I've decided to give you a stay of punishment."

Relief washed over K'lani in such a way that it almost
buckled her knees. Rayna caught her under the arm
before she fell over and helped her remain steady. K'lani
gripped Rayna's hand as a "thank you" knowing she
was the one who spoke to her father. Rather than lean
into revenge as she once would have, Rayna chose to
forgive K'lani for her actions and thus her father did as
well.

"I'm not finished," Kazu said.

Kemi came beside him and the two slowly made their
way down the steps of the dais until they faced K'lani.
Fear overcame her once again and she held fast to
Rayna's hand for comfort. Rayna gave her a light
squeeze but then let her go. K'lani stood on her own
again as her father made a last commandment over her
future.

"Because of your bravery in the face of magnificent
odds, I am granting you a place within the Khai soldiers
as you've requested."

K'lani couldn't believe what she was hearing. Not only

did her father not hand down punishment he rewarded her with something she had sought for many years. Being allowed to train with the Khai was a wonderful prize but she'd been granted something much better than that: her father's acceptance.

~

Rayna watched K'lani share a moment with her family. Even her father embraced his daughter. It was a joyous thing to see. Rayna didn't get a lot of those herself. So, she made sure K'lani received a pardon and proper recognition for her help.

Not only had she been vital to the destruction of Cebrios, but without K'lani's help on Atharia, the witch Nadiuska and her Daughters of Chaos would still be running amok. She also explained how K'lani had been responsible for escorting the spirit of Kemi's husband Valerios to the other side to find his peace. Emperor Kazu didn't want to hear from the outsider at first but with Zhayn and Kemi backing her up, Rayna got him to agree to terms.

A celebration was had that night to honor K'lani and everyone who helped defeat the God of Wind. They were lucky that his destructive path didn't reach the town or the palace. Now the people of Ischon could move forward in their future without leaning on a god who only placed his needs first.

Rayna stayed for the feast but when the dancing began, she excused herself from the hall. Outside under the calm night sky she sat with Ryu and watched from afar. The merriment of the festivities stretched from the palace outside into the streets. Everyone was in lively spirits after facing down death. Those that didn't make it out of the battle would be honored with a traditional ceremony.

It was a bittersweet ending to a long-fought war with the Source Gods. Now Rayna only had one last quest remaining before she could hang up her sword and settle down.

"Are you ready to go home?" she asked Ryu.

He nodded. Rayna felt weary but ready to go. If she opted to stay at the palace another night she may never leave. Ischon was not at all what she expected it to be. It was beautiful and comforting. Now that the people grew to know her intentions, they welcomed her with open arms. But this wasn't her home, nor was it Ryu's.

A promise had been made to his mother, and the black dragon Nazalon, to bring Ryu to the Isle of Dragons. There he could live among his kind without the threat of human poachers. With everything safely behind her, it was time Rayna honored that promise.

Before they headed out, Rayna made a point of saying farewell to K'lani. She found her in the middle of a celebratory dance with Zhayn. The way the two held each other told a thousand tales. Kemi came up alongside Rayna and the two of them watched the pair dancing together.

"Seems my little sister has been awarded more than just a place with the Khai."

"Indeed, it does," Rayna agreed. "It's nice to see her happy. I hope you find that happiness as well, Kemi."

"I will," she replied. "I've decided to take a more active role in the council. My father could use a variety of opinions rather than many voices simply speaking what he wants to hear."

"I'm sure you'll be fine."

"As will you."

Kemi took Rayna's hand and placed a small bag within her palm. It was soft to the touch as though filled with herbs. Rayna raised an eyebrow in question.

"A remedy for any malaise you may feel in the coming months," Kemi explained. "It's to be chewed not smoked."

Rayna tucked the bag away and thanked her. She glanced back out to the dance floor and saw Zhayn pull K'lani in for a kiss. Far be it for her to interrupt such a pure moment. Instead, she said her goodbyes to Kemi and told her to pass along a farewell to K'lani.

Leaving the palace, she climbed upon Ryu's back and headed out. The two of them took to the sky leaving Ischon behind as they sought an isle few knew existed.

26
Here There Be Dragons

They had no maps, no past explorations to draw from, not even Ryu's own instinct to guide them. Trying to find the Isle of Dragons proved almost impossible. Rayna wondered if it even existed at all. Perhaps when Nazalon told her to take the baby dragon there he only meant to provide her with purpose. Well, that baby had grown considerably in size since then. Their bond had grown as well.

At first, she wanted nothing more than to relieve herself of dragon-sitting duty. But the more time they spent together, surviving death, and exploring the world, the less she wanted to leave Ryu. But it wasn't up to her. If there were an Isle of Dragons out there, she owed it to him to provide a choice. Let Ryu make his own decision. First, they needed to find it.

They were too far from Ischon to turn back and Atharia's closest shores were even further away. Rayna was intent on finding a vast isle full of dragons. For now, she instructed Ryu to set down on the nearest patch of land.

He circled about until finding a small land mass in the distance. On Rayna's command they headed towards it. Better to set down and regroup before taking the long journey back to Atharia.

"Sorry, Ryu. We tried," she told him. "I'm starting to think that the Isle of Dragons doesn't even exist."

Flying closer to the small land mass proved Rayna wrong. It wasn't a single island mass but a cluster of them and they weren't small at all. Ryu picked up speed towards the largest of the islands and almost collided with a dragon of comparable size. She approached from the opposite side heading in the same direction they were though no rider guided her.

Ryu pulled himself up to avoid the collision causing Rayna to shift her balance on his back. As she moved the other dragon caught sight of her and began shrieking. To her surprise, Ryu yelled back. The two dragons seemed to be involved in an argument she couldn't understand. Then finally the other one backed off.

She flew on ahead with great speed leaving Ryu hovering in the air. The coloring of the dragon was unlike anything Rayna had ever seen before. Her skin looked bright as the sun with cobalt blue scales covering her breast. The surprise appearance caught Rayna off guard, and she needed time to contemplate their next move.

With the dragon sighting she knew her initial thoughts were wrong. The Isle of Dragons was close. They could follow the dragon's tail to find it. By now she was just a dark streak in the sky. Ryu headed after her anyway.

His large wings pulled through the air with admirable strength. Sometimes Rayna forgot he was still just a young dragon. He'd proven himself more than capable on many occasions. And all of this without any guidance from his own kind. Once Ryu was among them there was no telling what he was capable of.

They caught up to the golden dragon who had stopped just feet from the large land mass. She hovered there awaiting their approach. Rayna felt an uneasiness in the pit of her stomach. The gold dragon was baiting them. When they got close enough, she gave a strange call.

Ryu noted the melody and started to turn them around. He didn't have time to pick up speed before they became surrounded. Dragons came flying up from the island all around them in differing sizes, shapes, and colors. They boxed Ryu in and forced him to follow their movements. With a dragon on either side, they steered him towards the island. Rayna could do little but cling to his back as they finally made it to the Isle of Dragons.

27
Way of the Dragon

The Isle of Dragons was the most beautiful land Rayna had ever set foot on. Untouched by man, it remained in its natural state with lush green grass, massive redwood trees, and flowing streams all around the valley.

But without humanity inhabiting the isle it also meant no advancements were made. The Isle of Dragons was exactly that: an island meant for dragons. No towns or castles could be seen anywhere on the land as they descended. There was no housing at all save what Rayna recognized as dragon nests.

The dragon brigade stayed with them as they landed in the center of the island. There were far too many of them, all various sizes and strengths. Resistance would be futile. Ryu was still just a young dragon. These that surrounded them were full grown adults. Not only would he have no chance to fight against the others, but it would be an insult to their hierarchy.

Rayna had bested many dragons in her day, but she wasn't about to take on an entire pack. Besides, they weren't there to fight. There's was a quest only to reunite Ryu with his own kind. Now that they had found the Isle of Dragons, she needed to convince them no blood would be spilled.

A large dragon with rust-colored scales and eyes like copper stepped out of the pack. Age crept over him leaving tufts of white hair on his chin and cheeks. He towered over Ryu and doubled his size. Rayna had only seen one other that could rival such a massive dragon.

Nazalon, the elusive dark one who tucked himself away on Atharia. He told her to come to the Isle of Dragons where he could not venture himself. The dragons took exile very seriously and Nazalon was no longer welcome there. Rayna didn't feel very welcome either.

"You dare bring a human among us!" the ancient one shouted. "That is an insult to the way of the dragon."

This time when Rayna understood the dragon it didn't shock her quite as much. She replied relieved they could open a dialogue. "We mean no harm."

"I know who you are," the old one told her. "You're the dragonslayer. A murderer of our kind."

At his words, the other dragons began snapping their jaws and shouting. Rayna sensed them closing the circle around her and Ryu. Taking a chance, she dismounted then removed her sword and tossed it into the sand at her feet.

"I'm the dragonslayer no longer."

The golden dragon whom they chased spoke up with a harshness to her tone. "Just because you travel with the red one doesn't mean you're a friend to the dragons now."

"Silence, Tharamus" the ancient one shouted. "Let us hear what our young friend has to say. Why have you come here, youngling?"

Ryu shifted on his haunches uncertain of what to do. Rayna feared the spell cast down by Thealia, Goddess of Earth, still stung his throat. She tried to speak for him and regretted it. The old dragon blew a plume of smoke in the air so close it almost singed her skin.

"We've already heard from you, human."

Ryu stepped in front of Rayna and shielded her with his wings. Then he found his own voice as the pack of dragons stared him down.

"Leave her be."

"Finally, he speaks," Tharamus joked. "Now answer Dagamon's question."

The dragon pack was growing unruly. Even with the ancient one, Dagamon, leading the inquiry it seemed as though they didn't care what Ryu's answer would be. Rayna was an outsider to their lands, and they didn't want her there. Ryu's response would seal his own fate, not hers.

"All of the dragons on Atharia have been extinguished," Ryu began. "I came here to find more of my kind and learn the ways of the dragon clan. But now that I see how you behave, I'm no longer interested in the old ways."

His words stirred the dragons into a fit. Many of the younger ones flew into the air circling overhead and waiting to launch an attack. The others snapped their large jaws at both Ryu and Rayna. It took everything within her not to flinch. She must show no fear even in the face of overwhelming danger.

"You breached our shores with the dragonslayer on your back and now dare to insult your own kind," Dagamon said. "That grieves me, child."

"I'm not your child," Ryu replied defiantly.

By now the other dragons had settled. Several of them took positions behind Dagamon while others remained close to Ryu and his human companion.

"You're right," Dagamon told him. "You were the child of Saarath. A mighty dragon slain by the one you protect now even at your own detriment."

"It's hypocrisy!" Tharamus hissed.

The others stamped their feet in agreement. It kicked up enough dirt to cause Rayna a fit of coughs. This only pleased the dragons.

"If you want to be welcomed into your rightful place with us then there is a test to pass," Dagamon said.

Ryu's large eyes narrowed, intrigued by the proclamation. "Tell me what I must do."

"To prove your loyalty to us, you must avenge the death of our kind and kill the human!"

Rayna felt a jolt of fear cascade over her body. She'd not felt such overwhelming dread since seeing her very first dragon. Back then she was a child watching in terror as her childhood home burned to ash with her parents inside. She hunted the dragon responsible for years only to find out it was a witch, not a dragon, which destroyed her life.

But the path of carnage she left along the way wasn't something she could ignore. No matter the reason, Rayna slayed all the dragons on Atharia. The clan on the Isle was right to want repercussions for it. But Dagamon went one step further with his statement hoping to spur Ryu into action.

"She killed your mother."

"She is my mother!" Ryu argued. "And she is with child. I'm not going to kill her, and neither are you."

Rayna's mouth fell agape. She couldn't believe Ryu stood up for her against his own kind. And the revelation of her pregnancy was a surprise as well. Though now her growing queasiness made more sense. Instinctively, she covered her belly to protect her unborn baby. Ryu kept himself in front of Rayna while the rest of the dragons began to close in.

"It seems you've made your choice," Dagamon said. "Pity. If you won't kill the human, then you both die!"

They all came in unison. So many talons and teeth ripped at Ryu with many of them trying to get at Rayna as well. He had to tuck himself into a ball and wrap both wings around her to keep her safe. She fell to her knees scrambling blind on the ground in search of her sword. If they were going to fall that day, she would take a stand alongside her dragon companion. They'd go down fighting...together.

Rayna's fingertips touched the hilt of Bhrytbyrn just as the dragons began to peel Ryu's wings open. She sought the jewel to ignite fire upon the blade only to find it cracked. The dragon's had trampled it under their feet trying to tear Ryu asunder. Rayna did her best to swing the massive blade at them, but it did little against their heavily scaled bodies.

As the dragonslayer, she spent days in advance preparation seeking any weakness to exploit on her target. The dragons on the isle showed only one: group think. They all moved together as one unit without any consideration for an alternative attack.

While they each wanted to rip a piece off the arrogant, young dragon they failed to recognize one in their midst who didn't follow along. He stood out within the throng of dragons billowing his massive black wings like sails on a ship.

When Rayna saw the ash-colored scales of his head lift it stilled her own attack. Higher the dark dragon rose looking out over the scene. Blackened eyes stared down at the others ripping at one of their own. Nazalon wasn't pleased.

An angry roar burst up from his belly echoing across the expanse of the sky. As he called out, the rest of the dragons stopped their assault on Ryu and stepped away.

"Leave the youngling alone," Nazalon ordered. "I'm the one who instructed them to come here."

"You don't have a place on the Isle of Dragons," Dagamon reminded him. "What made you think they would?"

"Because you owe Saarath, fool!" Nazalon barked. "Yet, I come to find you've become nothing but a savage lot since she's been away."

"What do you expect us to do when he brings the dragonslayer into our midst and then sides with her?" Tharamus argued.

"I've seen the woman care for Ryu as if he were her own," Nazalon told them. "When she tells you she is slayer no more she speaks the truth."

As the dragon council shouted back and forth, Rayna checked on the damage Ryu took. He was scratched and beaten but otherwise alright. She rubbed his snout and tried to smile.

"You didn't have to protect me like that."

"After everything you've done for me, of course I did," he replied.

"I'm glad you're speaking to me again."

"What happened with my mother is not your fault," Ryu told her. "She asked you to watch over me and you did so...faithfully. Now I'm going to watch over you and the baby."

Rayna stroked her stomach again. "I can't believe I'm with child. How did you know?"

"I can sense these things."

Amid their discussion Rayna noted the other dragons had gone quiet. She looked up to find the lot of them staring down at she and Ryu. They were speaking in whispers among each other. Nazalon and Dagamon were in deep conversation as well.

"What're they saying?" Rayna asked, hand gripping tight to her sword.

"I don't know," Ryu replied. "But put that down. It won't do any good here."

Rayna opted to keep hold of her sword as the dragons gathered closer. She wondered how being burned alive would feel. Did the pain last until the body turned to ash or did one die the moment the flames overwhelmed them? She tried to shut out the morbid thoughts but the more she tried, the harder it became.

"I watched you there, caring for red Ryu," Dagamon said to her. "And he in turn protected you. It's a peculiar relationship, one I haven't seen in years."

"Human and dragon together? It's unheard of," Tharamus said.

"No, I've seen it," Dagamon explained. "Long ago before the lust for power split the world our kind slept, ate, and traveled alongside humans. We called them the dragon riders. It appears now some still share that unique bond."

"So, you'll grant them a pardon then?" Nazalon asked.

"Indeed, I will."

The dragon brigade began to grow rowdy at Dagamon's decision. As the oldest among them he only need bark to silence any who may challenge his rule. With the mighty Nazalon there to second his decision, the others didn't dare act out.

Rayna respected the way Nazalon helped them, at great risk to himself. It was the second time the dark dragon saved her life. She wanted to do something for him in return.

"What about Nazalon? Might you grant him a pardon as well?"

Dagamon couldn't help but laugh. "You are a feisty one, dragon rider. Very well, we shall also welcome back Nazalon into the fold."

This proclamation brought cheers from the group. Even

Ryu shouted out his pleasure. Nazalon seemed stunned, almost overwhelmed by emotion.

"I thank you," he told Dagamon. "And I thank you, Rayna."

In all her days of hunting dragons never did Rayna think she would wind up making peace with them. But here she stood surrounded by many now a welcome guest to the Isle of Dragons.

PART II

28

Dragon Born

Raven was the first human child born on the Isle of Dragons. Her mother, Rayna, never intended on staying on the isle for the birth. But the more time she spent with the dragons, the less she wanted to leave.

They were full of knowledge of the early days of the world. Dagamon especially knew his history. It gave Rayna a new appreciation for the world in which she, and now her daughter, walked on. It also gave her a better understanding of dragons.

For years all she saw them as were hunters. Vile, malicious being set on destroying anything in their path. But now she realized how layered their kind was. Even Ryu, whom she spent so much time with, surprised her with his wit.

Dagamon explained how the dragon developed their intelligence swiftly. He told her how their personalities developed based on their surroundings. Ryu was unique in that way. He'd spent most of his formative years with Rayna, picking up traits that were inherently human.

"He likes your kind," Dagamon told her. "In any other circumstance that would be extremely dangerous. But I can see the strength of the bond between the two of you. It really is quite remarkable, like the days of old."

So taken Dagamon was with Ryu's appreciation for his human that the last of the dragons there on the isle opted to name Rayna an honorary dragon rider. Her inclusion into the pack, along with Nazalon's insistence, brought her special treatment.

They set up a sleeping area for her and made sure she got enough to eat. After a while, Tharamus and the other females of the pack began to dote on Rayna. They could smell the infant growing in her belly and it set off their protective nature. Things had come full circle then. Rayna started her journey protecting a small baby dragon. Now the dragons watched over her baby daughter.

It was a quiet evening under a blanket of stars when word reached Rayna. A former suitor was asking about her back on Atharia, wondering if anyone knew where he could find her. Rayna's thoughts went to Jagger, her husband. She promised to return swiftly to him and once again she broke a promise.

Nazalon had been the one to bring her the news. He

often trekked back and forth from the Isle of Dragons to Atharia. Much like Ryu, he was caught between two worlds. Rayna knew Ryu had been enjoying himself there on the isle. He'd even made amends with Tharamus and was spending alot of time with her. Rayna didn't want to pull him away from everything. He was meant to have his peace. But she must return to Atharia with Raven. Jagger needed to meet his daughter.

"I need to go home now," she told Nazalon.

He nodded his large head. "I will take you. But you should say your goodbyes to the youngling."

Even the thought of saying goodbye to Ryu made Rayna tear up. She wiped her eye and bit her lip to keep it from quivering. Ryu didn't need to see her upset; it would only bring him sorrow.

He sat at the shoreline with Tharamus. Their tails linked together in a way that told Rayna something deeper than friendship stirred between the two young dragons. The usual sure-footed warrior stumbled through the trees making as much noise as possible. She wanted to relieve any embarrassment that may come from catching them off guard.

"Sorry to interrupt," Rayna said. "I need to have a word with Ryu. Tharamus, do you think you could help Nazalon watch over Raven? I'm not certain he knows how to care for a child."

"You'd be right about that," Tharamus replied.

She nuzzled her head under Ryu's chin then pushed past Rayna into the trees. Ryu dipped his head low to the ground so he could hear better. As he got closer to Rayna, he at once sensed something was wrong.

"Why are you crying?"

"I got sand in my eye."

"Now you're lying."

She knew better than to try and keep the truth from him. But the words were hard to say. Rayna needed to avert her gaze before she could tell Ryu the truth.

"It's time I go home," she said. "I'm here to say goodbye."

"Why would you need to say goodbye?" he asked. "If it's time to go, then I'm coming with you."

"No, Ryu," she said turning back to him. "Your place is here among your people."

"My place is with you. It always has been, and it always will be."

She stared back at the dragon, so big now since the first time she found him. They'd been through many battles together, surviving even when all hope seemed lost. The decision to stay or leave had always been up to Ryu. It seemed he'd made up his mind long ago and was just waiting for Rayna to make the call.

"I suppose any good dragon rider needs a dragon upon which to ride," she said with a smile.

Nazalon agreed to escort them back to Atharia. He

wanted to ensure nothing happened to either child, Ryu or Raven. The rest of the dragon clan bid their farewells. Dagamon reminded them they would be welcome on the Isle of Dragons anytime. Then they were off back to the shores of her homeland to reunite with Jagger.

"This man asking for me," she called to Nazalon as they flew. "Short cropped hair, striking features?"

"No," Nazalon told her. "He had a dark complexion. Looked to be a foreigner to Atharia though he asked for you by name."

Rayna shuddered at his words, and it woke baby Raven. She began to fuss. Rayna did her best to comfort the child while she felt little comfort herself. The former suitor Nazalon described was not Jagger. Dark features from a foreign shore told her Kartha. That could only mean one thing: somehow Toth had survived.

29
A Time of Ghosts

Even with the looming threat of danger in the air it still felt good to be home. Nazalon escorted them just to the outer edge of Atharia where Corinth sat. Then he turned back for the Isle of Dragons leaving Ryu to carry Rayna and baby Raven the rest of the way.

Corinth, and its surrounding area, had been a wasteland for many years. Rayna didn't expect any threats would come from the southern tip of Atharia. But if Toth regained his powers he could rise anywhere. With the threat of the God of Fire looming it made Rayna glad that she left the Isle of Dragons.

The Source Gods held immeasurable powers. Toth could've tracked her to the isle and decimated e very last dragon there. On Atharia, Rayna had a better chance of isolating him and containing any fallout that may affect the people.

She instructed Ryu to take them into Theopilous. There she would reunite with Jagger and leave Raven with him. It was difficult to navigate her warrior side with being a new mother. Rayna hoped when her daughter was born that she could leave the battles behind. Now she realized that would never happen. Her history as the slayer of dragons, witches, and gods would always bring trouble her way. Leaving Raven in her father's care was the only way to keep her safe.

"Shall I conceal myself in the Fickle Forest again?" Ryu asked.

"I'm sorry but it's for the best," Rayna told him. "If the people of Theopilous see you hovering over the town it will spark a panic. Some of them may even try to attack you."

"Very well, but I'll be close by should you need me."

Ryu let them off just a few feet from the gates of town. Rayna was thankful to have Ryu fly them over the Red Waste. Trying to endure the heat from the dry, desert wasteland would have have gone well with an infant in her arms.

She kept her baby in a papoose snuggled against her breasts. The closeness was a comfort for both as it replicated Raven's time in the womb. It also kept Rayna's hands free should she need to arm herself. Stepping into Theopilous she kept her sword sheathed and her other tools at her belt. In that town a drawn weapon meant an immediate altercation. Rayna only meant to find Jagger and be on her way. She knew he wouldn't like her leaving again but it was the only choice that made sense.

She sought Talos at his tavern. He knew both Rayna and Jagger well. If anyone could provide her with Jagger's whereabouts it would be Talos. Heading into the tavern she hoped the raucous nature of the patrons wouldn't disturb Raven too much. She tried to shield the baby's ears as well as she could. Heading straight for the bar, she located Talos there. His eyes lit up when he saw Rayna approach. When he caught sight of the baby, he couldn't contain his smile.

"Is she yours?"

Rayna gave a nod. Talos was so delighted with the news he did something uncustomary and bought a round of drinks for the entire tavern. It pained Rayna to push hers back but, as she told Talos, she was still feeding baby Raven from the breast.

"I never would've thought to see the day that Rayna, the mighty warrior, would have a little one to care for."

Rayna smiled. If Talos only knew she'd been caring for a small dragon for the better part of the year he may have had other thoughts. For a woman who lost her mother at a young age, Rayna grew into the role of caregiver quite well. When Raven began to fuss, it made Rayna cut to the quick of their conversation.

"I'm trying to locate Jagger. Do you know where he is?"

"I haven't seen him in a while," Talos told her. "But there was another man asking around about you. Tall guy, dark skin."

"He's here?!"

Her startled response caused Raven to start crying. Rayna tried to settle the baby, but her daughter could intrinsically sense her mother's upset. A crying baby in a tavern brought stares from judgmental eyes forcing Rayna to take her leave. With Toth sniffing around Theopilous to try and find her it no longer felt safe within the town. She would take her child and Ryu further inland away from any towns.

Routing her way to the Fickle Forest, Rayna called out for Ryu. Regardless of the fables that gave the wooded area its name, she still didn't want to venture too deep inside. Wolves and bears were very real. She'd rather avoid taking Raven towards a legitimate threat. But when calling out for Ryu didn't bring the dragon out, there was little other choice. Rayna started inside Fickle Forest with her baby in one arm and her sword in the other.

30
Old Haunts

S hadows fell across the forest floor playing tricks on Rayna's eyes. The mass of thick palm fronds that grew there blotted out the sun making it appear to be dusk at all hours. Baby Raven finally stopped fussing enough for Rayna to slip her back inside the cotton papoose.

Edging deeper inside the Fickle Forest, Rayna tried to call out for Ryu again. Her voice echoing on the trees made Raven fidget. Better to let sleeping babies lay. A dragon of Ryu's size would be hard to miss. That is, if he remained inside the forest. He could've left to find food or else been drawn out by Talos.

Dark thoughts plagued her mind, and she became desperate to find him. Even though he was almost a full-sized dragon and speaking now she still saw him as a youngling. The same would happen when her daughter grew up. No matter how big or bold they got, Rayna would never stop protecting them.

She pushed past a bramble of vines and branches into a clearing. Here she recalled the first time Jagger entered her life again. She'd been tasked by the royal guard on the order of King Favian. Rayna led the king's odious son through the Fickle Forest only to have Jagger and his band of mercenaries try and rob them.

This time when she entered the clearing, she found her dragon. Ryu lay on the ground with dirt covering half his torso. Rayna rushed to his side checking for wounds to care for. As her fingers grazed his scales Ryu came awake. Startled at first, he jerked his head back. But upon seeing Rayna, he greeted her with a massive yawn.

"What're you doing?" she asked.

"I was sleeping."

"Buried in dirt?"

"It's how I get comfortable by rooting around."

"You looked dead."

Ryu chuffed causing a small ring of smoke to plume from his nostrils. "Nothing on this land can harm me."

"That's not entirely true," Rayna told him. "Toth is back."

Ryu shifted up onto his haunches. "How?"

"I don't know. Maybe I was foolish enough to believe I actually defeated a Source God." Rayna shrugged. "Maybe they're all back."

"No, I ripped Thealia apart myself," Ryu argued. "They can't be back."

"They can and they are."

"What should we do?"

"We can't stay out here exposed. I know a place where we can go to regroup."

They headed out towards the farmlands in the northern region of Atharia. There sat a farmhouse tucked away from prying eyes. Rayna frequented the spot when she needed a place to stay. The original owner, Josep, was a kindly old man who allowed Rayna room and board. He'd since passed away but with no heirs to take up the land, it sat empty. Rayna only hoped that through the passage of time it hadn't become occupied.

Ryu flew them the entire way. Soaring over the giant wall that was the dragon's backbone, Rayna saw just how tall it truly stood. He turned and followed the Watersnake River straight into the farmland. Golden fields of wheat covered the land swaying in unison as Ryu touched down.

Josep's farmhouse was just down the path. It looked run down with faded wood and worn roofing. The barn had collapsed signaling that no animals remained on the property. It looked abandoned.

"It doesn't appear anyone is staying here," Rayna said.

"Good for us," Ryu replied. "I'll check out the barn, you head up to the house."

The place appeared abandoned, but something felt heavy in the air. Rayna trusted her instincts and took extra caution before entering. She shifted baby Raven's papoose to her back to provide more protection then edged inside slowly.

Opening the door provided a small bit of light into an otherwise darkened interior. The windows were boarded up leaving only slits between the wood to look through. A scarce amount of furniture was arranged in a way that provided defense from projectile attacks.

By the time Rayna realized the house wasn't abandoned, the squatter already got the jump on her. He lunged at her with a knife that almost caught her cheek. Fortunately, the assailant's moves were sloppy. It gave Rayna the opening to avoid the blow.

In the dim of the light, she just barely made out the silhouette of a man. He was lean and quick, armed with a curved dagger that he swung at her face again. Rayna angled herself out of the way again. This time she noted the grip of the man's hand on his weapon was lax. His hands shook from an uncontrollable twitch caused by damage to flesh and nerves. Recognizing her attacker, she cried out for him to stop.

"Jagger, it's me!"

He took another step forward before her voice registered in his ears. Then he dropped the dagger. Rayna pulled the front door open fully so the sunlight could spread through the room. It fell across Jagger's face highlighting a broken man full of despair. His skin looked gaunt with dark circles under his eyes. A full beard covered his chin and his hair had grown out again.

Jagger looked at her in disbelief. He trailed a shaky hand through her blonde locks lightly tugging at one of the braids. By now the commotion had upset Raven. She started to cry which made Jagger take a step back.

"What is that?" he asked. "Did you find another baby dragon?"

Rayna shook her head. "No, this is our baby."

She shifted the papoose around and lifted Raven out of it. She fussed and kicked until her bright blue eyes fell upon her father. Her chubby cheeks pinked up as she smiled his way.

"Do you want to hold her?" Rayna asked.

Jagger reached out but upon seeing his hands shake he pulled away. "I can't."

"I will help you," Rayna told him.

Jagger sat in a wooden chair set up by the cold, stone fireplace. Rayna set the baby in his arms and helped him to hold her there. He sat staring at her until the girl reached a tiny hand up and pulled at his beard.

"Ouch, little one," Jagger told her softly.

"Raven. I named her Raven."

"I like that," he said, smiling at Rayna. "She's really mine?"

A pang of curiosity twisted Rayna's stomach but only for a moment. She knew in her heart Raven was Jagger's child. They shared the same eyes, the same mischievous spirit. Even if there were a morsel of a chance that he wasn't the father, she wasn't going to indulge it.

"Yes, she's your daughter."

"Take her," he demanded.

Surprised by his sudden change in demeanor, Rayna took the child. Jagger walked to the open door. For a moment, Rayna thought he might leave. But he stood looking out at the sun as it began to fade.

"What's wrong?" she asked. "Why are you out here all alone?"

"I had nowhere else to go," he replied. "But I should've been with you, wherever you were, I should've been there to see my child born."

"You're here now, Jagger. And I need you. We both do. I need you to care for Raven."

"Where are you running off to this time?"

Rayna walked to him and rested her hand upon his shoulder. "Nowhere tonight. I'm exhausted and we really need to get some rest."

Jagger turned round and hugged them both. Then he glanced a kiss off Rayna's forehead which prompted Raven to coo until she received one as well.

"I saw Ryu out there scrounging for food," Jagger said. "I'm afraid he won't find much."

"He's resourceful," Rayna told him. "I'm sure he'll be fine."

"There's not much here for a baby to eat either," he replied. "In the morning, I'll fetch her something. For now, I just want to be with my little family."

Rather than climb the worn-out stairs up to the bedrooms they opted to sleep on the floor. Rayna put together a makeshift cradle with what she could find among the furniture. A lot of what Josep originally dressed the place with had either rotted or been destroyed by Jagger in a drunken stupor. It wasn't a lot but it was enough for the baby to get snuggled.

Rayna and Jagger set piles of blanket and furs upon the floor and then lay next to each other. She remembered the last time they were at the farmhouse together. They'd made love with a passion that only came when one expected their death was imminent.

That night Rayna just lay against his body letting the warmth of him seep into her. Soon they slept. Both too worn out and exhausted to recognize the approach of intruders outside.

31
The King of Atharia

At night they came by the dozens. First, they took the dragon, pinning him down with ropes and chains. Then they moved inside. Each action made with speed, accuracy, and silence. Rayna didn't realize they were upon her until she was being dragged halfway out the door.

Struggling against her captors caused them to stumble. They lost their grip on her but only for a moment. When she tried to run one caught her hair and yanked her back while another took her around the waist. Lifting her in the air, they slammed Rayna into the ground and held her there while her hands and feet were bound.

From her vantage point she saw them do the same to Jagger. Large men with bronzed skin covered in paint hovered over both. In the faintest of moonlight, Rayna couldn't make out the colors. These men could be from any tribe come to claim the mighty slayer and her dragon. Or they stumbled upon the farmhouse and sought any spoils inside. Whatever the case, Rayna and the others were at their mercy.

~

They were gagged, blind folded, and put into wagons. Rayna feared for her baby. Raven had yet to cry out making it difficult to tell where she was. Anytime Rayna tried to speak through the gag she received an open-hand slap across the cheek.

Rather than continue to get beaten, she opted to work on the binds tying her hands and feet. Whatever technique these men used was impossible to break. They looped an extra bit of rope between her hands and feet so that each time she moved it would pull her from either direction. It was a frustrating predicament. Rayna defeated witches and Source Gods only to be defeated by a piece of twine.

When struggling against her binds started to chafe her wrists she stopped. Better to use her other skills to try and discern how much trouble they were in. The men used wagons for transport rather than horses alone. That meant they were well funded. Noises outside the wagon were limited meaning they took back roads away from towns.

A scent of the ocean hung in the air that was very familiar to Rayna. The wagon shifted and turned closer to the scent which told her they were somewhere by the sea. Then she remembered. Saltwood Stronghold stood close to the Ship's Haven where boats were docked for transport across the sea. Were they abducted by pirates looking to fetch a price for their sale? It wouldn't be the first time.

The wagons slowed and then halted. She heard the men outside speaking though everything was muffled. Light shone on her face as the curtain to the wagon drew back. Warmth came with it indicating torch light rather than sunlight. They traveled quite a distance but not far enough for morning to breach the night.

Strong arms pulled Rayna from the wagon and marched her. With her feet bound it was difficult to walk let alone try to run away. Her captors made certain she wasn't going anywhere except where they led her. They walked up cobblestone steps, through a doorway, and into a vast room. Each step of their nail-down boots echoed in what sounded like a great hall.

Now Rayna knew where they were. They'd taken her to Saltwood Stronghold. She'd been inside the castle enough to recognize its familiar sounds and scents. What she didn't know was who had taken her. The last king on the throne, King Falkon, died in front of her eyes. Whomever took his place in the time she was away from Atharia seemed just as foul as Falkon had ever been.

Her captors led her to what she recognized as the

throne room. They dropped her to the ground letting her fall knees first. She heard a thud next to her indicating Jagger was dropped as well. Then a voice called out.

"Remove the blindfold. She only has one good eye anyway."

Rayna recognized who gave the order. As the coverings were removed, she wasn't surprised to find Talakai standing before her though his demeanor had changed.

He wore a long, white tunic made of silk and embroidered with gold thread. Since Rayna last saw him, Talakai collected more jewels to wear upon his fingers and around his neck. His humble crown was replaced with one adorned with ornate jewels. Like many kings before him, he'd gone power mad.

"Lovely to see you again, Rayna," he said with a smile.

"So, you're the tall, dark, foreign man who has been looking for me," she replied. "This is the second time you've had me taken against my will just for conversation. In the future, you can just ask."

He strode over and grabbed her by the chin. "I'm not here to talk. I'm here to take. You told me when you left Kartha that I should rule my people and rebuild. Well, I have. I rebuilt an army and, noting that Atharia had no true king upon the throne, I took it. Saltwood Stronghold is no more. This is the new Krato Castle!"

"Who is this ass?" Jagger asked. He received a strike to

the temple for the insult.

"I am Talakai, the King of Kartha, and your new ruler of Atharia."

"You can't just appoint yourself king," Rayna argued.

"I can and I did. I took the crown and now I'm going to take you as my queen." He paused, a look of pure disdain creasing his brow. "Oh, and I'll be taking my baby as well."

His words riled up Jagger who got another strike for his efforts. Rayna wanted to rip out Talakai's throat with her teeth. Instead, she tried to hurt him with words.

"She's not your baby."

"Nonsense. The infant is new to this world. Given the time we were together that makes her my child. How dare you try to hide her from me!"

With that, Talakai slapped Rayna across the face. Her flesh stung from the blow but not as much as the threat of losing her baby to a madman. She couldn't help but wonder now if Talakai requested her help to defeat Toth so it would make way for his world domination.

"Where is my baby?" she asked, blood spilling from a split lip. "Where is my dragon?"

"The dragon I'm going to have killed. The baby is coming with me," Talakai spoke in matter-of-fact terms. "Now, you can either rot away the rest of your days in the dungeon or choose to be my queen. If you conform and do your duties as a I see fit, I'll spare your dragon and you will of course help raise our daughter."

Seeing no other way out of the mess Rayna agreed. Once she had Talakai's word that Ryu and Jagger were safe, she would go about relieving him of his crown and his head. For now, there was no other way. Except Jagger had ideas of his own.

"I've got claim to that child, Talakai," he said.

"In what manner?"

"She's my daughter, not yours."

Talakai looked between Rayna and Jagger with disgust. "You bedded this nobody? He looks like a homeless man."

"Jagger is my husband, you fool," Rayna said. "I told you about him before."

"Well, this is a bit of a predicament." Talakai paced the floor trying to come up with a solution that served him. "I am a man who honors custom. Thus, the reason I've asked for your compliance, Rayna, rather than just violating you at my pleasure."

"I'll fight you for her," Jagger said.

His suggestion pleased Talakai but not Rayna. She knew with Jagger's injuries he would be no match for Talakai. Jagger always had a plan based on his wits but this time he ran on emotion. It was going to get him killed.

"Very well, I accept your challenge," Talakai said.

His eagerness told Rayna he knew Jagger's weakness. It

made her speak out.

"I'm not going to have you fight over me like some prize," she argued. "I'll fight for myself."

Talakai shook his head. "Your husband made the challenge and I have accepted. We shall battle for your hand in marriage. You can't very well marry yourself, foolish girl."

He turned to his guards, which Rayna now recognized as the Royal Watchers. Those who grabbed them in the night with such skill must've come from the Spirit Watcher tribe. Talakai did indeed bring his entire army to Atharia. He was quite serious about taking over and even more serious about fighting Jagger.

32
Spirit of Competition

Since taking over as ruler, Talakai wanted to make everything a spectacle. The battle between him and Jagger was set up so the people could watch their new king in action. They brought in seats and circled them around the training pits where the soldiers usually practiced the arts of war.

While they prepped for the fight it gave Rayna a chance to talk Jagger out of going. He had been placed down in the cells while Talakai prepared in his chambers. Rayna was allowed to walk freely though the ever-present shadow of the Royal Watchers remained at her back.

She thought about taking them out and fleeing from the grounds. But that would entail breaking Jagger from his cell, locating Raven, and releasing Ryu from his binds. It would be one against an army with so much more to lose if she failed.

A small cutaway in the main door to the cells allowed food to be passed through. Rayna used it to converse with Jagger. He slipped his hand out and she took it within her own. She could feel the nerves twitch within his arms no matter how hard he tried to control them.

"You can't do this, he'll kill you."

"Please, I've handled worse than a perfumed prince like that."

"But you were at your best then."

"So, now you've lost faith in me?"

"Of course not. But your hands...."

"Rayna, a little shake in my palms isn't going to stop me from destroying this idiot," he told her. "I'm going to get our daughter back."

She wanted to tell him so much more. "I love you" felt weak compared to the depth of what Jagger meant to her. She held onto his hand, and they sat in silence until it was time to fight. The guards forced Rayna out as Jagger got ready. They led her to a parapet where Talakai awaited.

"Aren't you going to give me a kiss for good luck?"

She looked him over in disgust. He wore form-fitted dark armor with matching greaves and fur-lined boots. The sword he carried into battle was her own. She gritted her teeth in such anger it hurt her jaw.

"I'll never touch you."

"After I kill your current husband in front of all to see,

you won't have a choice."

Talakai forced a kiss on her then pushed her out of the way. The Royal Watchers led her to the box where she would watch the fight. Outside under the fresh morning air, the town of Sandhal and other neighboring properties gathered to watch. None of them knew the ramifications if Talakai was victorious.

Jagger stepped out first. He wore light armor with dual knives at his belt. Because of his condition, he chose freedom of movement over protection. Knives would be easier to hold than a heavy sword. Rayna knew he was well-trained with many styles of weaponry. She could only hope it would be enough.

Talakai entered next to a fanfare of trumpets. Servant girls threw rose petals at his feet. He waved to the crowd, and they ate up every moment of his pageantry. The kind young man she knew had fallen away to reveal a narcissist. Perhaps his arrogance would be his undoing.

After long, drawn out words from Krato Castle's new wiseman the battle began. Talakai danced around at the start, playing with Jagger. To Jagger's credit, he didn't rush in with a head full of rage. He took his time and waited for the king to make a mistake.

That mistake came when he stepped a little too close. Once in range, Jagger lashed out with both knives at once. The sweeping pattern caused Talakai to duck and move with great agility. Rayna felt a gulp of air catch in her chest.

Talakai held great control over his body. He was far more skilled than she expected. Frustration with his ailment caused Jagger to lunge in with a haphazard strike. He was trying to finish the fight before he could no longer hold his weapon. The sloppy movement allowed Talakai an opening to return with his own attack.

Using Rayna's own broadsword, he slashed Jagger across the shoulder. Fortunately, he managed to turn just enough that most of the blade caught his armor and not flesh. Still, a cut tore into the meat of his arm and it caused him to drop one of the knives.

Seeing this, Talakai sought to end him. He double gripped the broadsword and swung high overhead. Jagger rolled beneath the attack and came up holding a clump of sand. He tossed it at Talakai's face causing the king to turn away.

Rayna lurched forward in her seat with excitement. Jagger knew the tricks he needed to employ to win the fight. The crowd turned on him with hisses and jeers, but it didn't matter. In a fight to the death, one did everything possible to survive.

With Talakai momentarily blinded, Jagger went in for the kill. He thrust forward with his remaining knife only to have it parried. Talakai hadn't been blinded at all. He used the tactic to draw Jagger in and when he had his opening he struck.

Bhrytbyrn cut through the thin armor and plunged deep into Jagger's stomach. His eyes went wide, and he spat blood across the hot sand. Talakai continued to drive the blade deeper, pushing him backwards until they both fell over.

33
Burn Them All

Rayna didn't even realize she was standing until the Royal Watcher tried to force her back down. She reacted with swift and blinding violence striking each one in the eyes and throat. With the guards out of her way, Rayna leapt from the box landing in a deep squat inside the makeshift arena.

More guards were heading her way, but she found help from some in the crowd. They remembered how the dragon warrior liberated them from the spell of the chaos witch and they repaid their debt by causing an obstruction. With the Royal Watchers momentarily distracted, Rayna rushed to the fallen fighters.

A swift kick knocked Talakai from atop Jagger, but it was too late. His eyes stared up at the sky looking at nothing. He was gone. Rayna fell to her knees within the blood that pooled beneath Jagger's body. She let herself cry for only a moment before rage took over.

Clutching Bhrytbyrn, she pulled it from the body of her dead husband and went to war with the so-called new king of Atharia. Talakai met her attack with Jagger's sand trick. He tossed a clump of dirt towards Rayna with intent on blinding her. She simply turned her face and allowed the grains of it to bounce off her eyepatch. Then she continued her advance.

But Talakai wasn't yet done. He moved with such speed; Rayna had a tough time catching up to him. Each time she swung her sword he avoided contact. Finally, she feigned a strike causing him to dodge the incoming blow. Instead, Rayna adjusted her footing and torqued her body with such force it cut Talakai's head clean from his shoulders.

Her momentum was so great, the sword strike pulled her to the ground with Talakai's fallen body. By now, the Royal Watchers pushed through the crowd and came for her. Rayna stood up, ready to hold them off or die trying. They drew their swords as they ran in then abruptly fell back with terror filling their eyes. A massive shadow cast over the sand and it was then that Rayna knew Ryu came for her. Whatever bonds they kept on him would be useless the moment he sensed she was in danger.

He swooped down into the middle of the square and growled at the lot of them. His anger was such that Rayna needed to draw back his dragon's fire lest he burn the town and everyone in it.

"Keep them back while I find Raven."

Rayna hurried inside the castle with a sense of dread weighing heavily on her shoulders. She shouted for her girl knowing the baby couldn't answer but continued calling regardless. A flash of a memory fell on her mind as she continued searching.

Early on when Ryu was still a baby dragon, she'd lost him in a field. Rayna called out in a panic trying to find him. Though he couldn't yet speak, he shouted back until she located him. The same thing occurred now. Raven began crying loud enough for Rayna to find her in a separate chamber off the throne room. Relieved, she cradled the girl in her arms and hurried back out to Ryu.

By then, the Spirit Watchers had gathered in a futile attempt to revenge their king. They threw spears at Ryu trying to overwhelm him so they could press in and strike a killing blow. Rayna cut down a few of them as she rushed by. Ryu offered her his tail for an easy climb onto his back.

With the dragon distracted, the Spirit Watchers advanced their attack. They pelted him with heavy stones swung on rope. A few of their blades cut deep in the soft spots of his body. Rayna noted the townspeople had dispersed leaving only the king's army behind. She leaned in and gave Ryu freedom to act.

"Burn them!"

On her word, Ryu ignited the lot of them. They went

up like fresh torches as his dragon fire enveloped their bodies. As the guards screamed and ran in panic, Rayna urged Ryu to go. He spread his wings and took to the sky. But they would not leave without first taking the castle down as well. Ryu sent bursts of fire into the structure and then launched his own body through it until it began to crumble.

Rayna looked back to watch the castle turn to dust. She scanned the grounds seeking Jagger's body but couldn't make it out. It pained her to look away, but baby Raven's crying took her attention. Once she settled the girl and looked back again, Ryu had taken them out across the ocean. Atharia was nothing but a memory to them now. They would not return that way again.

34
Legacy of the Dragon

Treading back into the Shadowed Highlands brought up memories Rayna would've preferred forgetting. At least this time she had people she could trust with her not a pack of ruthless soldiers. Coraise was the exception. If his true wits were about him he would've tried to escape by now.

Rayna sat outside watching the water churn in the river as Raven fished nearby. Over a decade had gone by since they settled on Ischon. Emperor Kivu Kazu passed peacefully in his sleep leaving his daughter Kemi to lead in his place. K'lani and Zhayn married and had a fine son and a beautiful daughter.

Even Ryu was expecting a little one of his own. He'd journeyed back and forth from Ischon to the Isle of Dragons to see Tharamus. The two of them had come together to prove the legacy of the dragons would live on.

Rayna built a small hut down by the water. It was close enough to the palace but far enough away to give them privacy. Raven enjoyed growing up there. Under Kemi's decree she was welcome to learn in their schools and even trained studied with the Wind Raiders. She was growing into a fine young woman.

Even with all that occurred in the last few years there wasn't a day that went by in which Rayna didn't think of Jagger. He was a good man and a legendary warrior who deserved a better fate than he got. Rayna would often sit outside while Raven played and reminisce about the times she shared with Jagger.

On this day, K'lani came to join her. She brought her little ones to play with Raven. They ran around with carefree zest and childlike innocence. It made Rayna smile.

"I haven't seen that smile in years," K'lani said sitting next to her.

"It's nice that they have each other," Rayna told her.

"Yes, it is."

K'lani patted her hand as though to infer it was nice that they had their friendship as well. Rayna nodded and continued looking out at the everlasting sky. As the sun began to set it cast an array of rich color over the horizon. Rayna couldn't help but think it was Jagger saying hello.

"Do you ever think of going back to Atharia?" K'lani asked her.

"There's nothing for me there," Rayna replied. "But perhaps someday I'll venture out to see what's beyond."

"Always the adventurer. Until then, why don't you write down some of the things you're always pondering. It will be a nice gift for Raven one day."

K'lani handed her a small booklet of paper that looked similar to the one she often carried. Rayna wasn't much for words and stories but jotting down her memories of Jagger would help Raven know her father.

She took a quill and started from the beginning....

END OF VOLUME III

I hope you enjoyed *Rayna the Dragon Rider* as much as I enjoyed writing it. Please leave a review at your favorite online retailer.

Reviews help authors maintain momentum with our writing by letting us know which types of stories are resonating. Plus, writing is a very isolating career and I really enjoy hearing feedback from readers!

Special Excerpt
Rise of the Dragonslayer
A Time of Dragons Prequel
Copyright © 2022 Cynthia Vespia

Rayna did not flinch as the ash rained down around her. She did not cry out nor run when the flames grew too hot. Only a single tear tumbled across her cheek, cutting a path through the dark soot on her skin.

Her other eye, the cursed one, remained dry as the girl watched her home engulfed in flames. It was as if she were two different halves experiencing the traumatic event in alternating ways. One cried out for her parents still trapped inside the house. The other reveled at the sight of splintered wood and a bowed roof swallowed up by the fire.

The last actions of her mother were to get Rayna out of harm's way. She told the girl to run and not stop until she reached the far village where her aunt and uncle lived. Rayna could still hear the words of her mother in the air telling her she'd be close behind. She never made it out of the house.

Rayna ran as instructed, but turned back when her mother did not join her. Her last memory was seeing the dark dragon burning her home. Then it took to the skies on leathery wings, leaving Rayna's life in ruins.

Her feet would not move as her one strange eye kept watch on the house until the fire smoldered. Once the flames flickered out, Rayna had to force her gaze from the ruin of her childhood home. Even then, the cursed eye wanted to see more. But Rayna would not submit to its wants this time. She found her eyepatch in the dirt at her feet and slipped it over her belligerent eye to calm it down.

She thought about going back into the wreckage to find her parents. They would be nothing but charred remains, their bones black as coal. It didn't matter, Rayna wanted to hold them one last time. But then she heard others coming. The neighboring houses, from a click over, must've seen the large plumes of smoke. They would know that Rionar, Kathyrn, and little Rayna were the only ones who lived out this way.

Others would come to see the mess from the fire. Then they would see Rayna standing there unscathed and they would cast the blame on her. The strange girl with the monstrous eye would be an easy scapegoat. When the scuffle of their boots grew too close, and the chatter of concern too loud, that is when Rayna finally ran.

Find out how it all started in Rise of the Dragonslayer!

Read it for FREE when you sign up for the newsletter at www.CynthiaVespia.com

Author's Note:

Will A Time of Dragons continue?

The short answer is I don't know. In my head, I toyed with writing a series of six books. But as the stories developed, they took unexpected turns that culminated in what I feel is the end of Rayna's journey with Ryu. If anything, a new adventure may come to light which follows Rayna and Jagger's daughter Raven and her adventures.

As a fun behind-the-scenes fact, I named the daughter Raven because I drew inspiration for my series from a wonderful group of fantasy novels by an author named Richard Kirk. Each of his five books in the series follows a female warrior by the name of Raven. I named Rayna's daughter this to pay homage to those books.

My A Time of Dragons series came to life originally because I saw a statue online of a beautiful but fierce warrior woman who had just slayed a dragon. On top of that, The Mandalorian had just come out on Disney. I thought to myself, wouldn't it be interesting if a woman who has been slaying dragons her entire life suddenly has to protect one? Thus, the story begins.

Book 3, Rayna the Dragon Rider, was meant to be something entirely different. But after dragons and witches where else can you go but merciless gods? The very ending with the pregnancy and the Talakai's return came to me as I was writing Rayna's battles with these fierce gods.

I liked the full-circle aspect of, not only the beginning of the book, but the entire series which really starts in the prequel. Jagger became a much bigger fixture in Rayna's life than even I realized he was going to be. Killing him was hard on all of us.

My initial intent with A Time of Dragons was to tell a true fantasy story grounded in the world of the pulp classics like Conan. I've only written sword & sorcery one time before with my Demon Hunter and Demon Huntress series respectively. This time, I really wanted to get my hands dirty with the world-building, hence the map!

I don't write epics, but I am pleased that readers have taken to the characters and enjoyed the ride with them. So, will there be any more A Time of Dragons novels?

You tell me....

Appendix

Names:
Rayna (Rain-ah)
Bhrytbyrn (bright-burn)
K'lani (Kay Lan E)
Valerios (Val-air-e-ous)
Favian (Fay-vee-an)
Falkon (Falcon)
Atharia (Ah-thar-e-ya)
Pelanor Pass (Pel-ay-nor)
Ischon across the Sea (E-shawn)
Emperor Kivu Kazu (Kee-Voo Kah-zoo)
Theopilous (Thee-op-ilous)
Valeuki (Val-ooh-kai)
D'zdario Dizdar (Diz-dar-e-o Diz-dar)
Tanoa'i (Tah-noh-AH ee)
Karithik (Car-ith-ick)
Laihaka Valley (Lie-hack-ah)
Talakai (Tal-uh-kai)
Nadiuska (Nad-e-ooh-ska)
Saarath (Sar-rath)
Persea (Per-say-uh)
Cebrios (See-bree-os)
Thealia (Thee-al-e-uh)
Zhayn (Zain)
Captain Khadan (Kay-dan)
Nazalon (Naz-ah_lon)
Tharamus (There-a-muss)
Dagamon (Dag-ah-mon)

About the Author

"Original Cyn" Cynthia Vespia writes fantasy novels with bite including urban fantasy vigilantes and heroic adventure fantasy. Her books have featured a secret group of superhero renegades; the dark side of vigilante justice in Las Vegas; and a duo of demon hunters fighting supernatural beings. Her latest venture is an exciting adventure series about a dragonslayer who has a change of heart.

Cyn received a "Best Series" nomination for her fantasy trilogy Demon Hunter. Her novel Karma ranked #1 on Amazon twice in several distinct categories including superhero, action-adventure, and contemporary fantasy. She has been published in anthologies such as Skelos Press and Dark Eclipse.

Her characters are outcasts and anti-heroes with depth

and real vulnerabilities. Each novel plot is designed to give heroes a challenge and villains a purpose. The worlds Cyn creates are a gritty mix of fantasy, magic, and the supernatural while exploring the theme of "success through struggle." She's expanded this theme into personal development books and guides.

Cyn has also written content for Microsoft, UFC, WWE, HBO, Netflix, and more. As a former fitness competitor she enjoys keep active through training. Cynthia is available for conventions, interviews and workshops.

Sign up for the newsletter and receive the Time of Dragons prequel Rise of the Dragonslayer for free
https://www.cynthiavespia.com/free-story

Follow on Bookbub:
https://www.bookbub.com/authors/cynthia-vespia

Follow on Facebook:
https://www.facebook.com/originalcynwrites

Follow on Instagram: @originalcynwrites

Follow on Youtube:
https://www.youtube.com/c/OriginalCynContent

Books by Cynthia Vespia

SILKES STRIKE FORCE

(superhero urban fantasy)

Karma

Kobra

Kaged

Khaos

VEGAS VIGILANTES

(dark urban fantasy)

Casino Empire

Lucky Sevens

Vegas Valkyrie

Sin City Assassin

DEMON HUNTERS

(heroic adventure fantasy)

Demon Hunter Saga

Demon Huntress Legends

OTHER BOOKS

The Crescent

Theater of Pain

Sins and Virtues

NONFICTION

Be Your Own Superhero